Dashing Through The Snow

Laura Rush

Copyright© 2024 Laura Rush

All rights reserved.

No part of this book may be reproduced in any form or by any electronic or mechanical means, including information storage and retrieval systems, without written permission from the author, except for the use of brief quotations in a book review.

This book is a work of fiction. All names, characters, locations, and incidents are products of the author's imagination or used in a fictional manner. Any resemblance to actual persons, living or dead, or actual events is purely coincidental.

Cover Designer Paperback – Laura Rush

Editing- Colby Bettley @novelandnoted

Formatting– Laura Rush

Contents

Jingle My Bell Series	1
Trigger Warnings	2
Playlist	3
Dedication	4
Chapter 1	5
Chapter 2	10
Chapter 3	17
Chapter 4	22
Chapter 5	26
Chapter 6	33
Chapter 7	38
Chapter 8	43
Chapter 9	49
Chapter 10	55
Chapter 11	61
Chapter 12	65
Chapter 13	75

Chapter 14	82
Chapter 15	88
Epilogue	94
Author Note.	99
Also, out by Laura Rush	100
Chapter 1 - Shaun	101
Chapter 2 - Brimley	105
Chapter 3 - Shaun	108
Chapter 4 - Brimley	110
Chapter 5 - Shaun	114
What's to Come.	119
Acknowledgements	121
About the Author	123

Jingle My Bell Series

Six sisters, six stories.... Interconnected Standalones.

Book 1 – So, This is Christmas – Out NOW on Amazon KU (Brimley's Story)

Book 2 – Dashing Through The Snow – Out NOW on Amazon KU (Franny's Story)

Book 3 – Coming November 2025 (Annie's Story)

Book 4 – Coming November 2026

Book 5 – Coming November 2027

Book 6 – Coming November 2028

Trigger Warnings

This story contains scenes you may find upsetting.

Please see below before continuing...

Anxiety, panic attacks and sexually explicit scenes are in this novel; aged 18+ is advised.

Playlist

Music to listen to while reading this book.

Dedication

Here's to broken bikes, and the enchantment of the night.
You never know when love might show, to make your world so bright!
To everyone who believes in the magic of the season – May your heart find it's way home for Christmas.

Chapter 1

Francesca - 32 years old.

The front tyres of my motorbike crunch over the freshly fallen snow before coming to a stop in front of Heath Fletcher's house. The chilly winter air whirls around me, gently frosting up the tip of my nose as I pull off my helmet.

A grin spreads across my face, and I can't help it.

The front of Heath's home always manages to bring a smile to my face, even at this ridiculous hour. It's deep blue painted exterior and white shutters give it a modern edge to the street it sits on.

The bushes that are planted in the borders at front of the house twinkle with fairy lights and a row of gnomes—dressed in Christmas outfits, no less—guard the three steps that lead up to his dark wooden door.

No matter the season, Heath's house always stands out from the rest of the neighbourhood. *Just like him, I guess.*

No other man has ever captured my heart the way he has.

Smart, caring, and just the right amount of dirty.

If you asked for my opinion, guys like Heath are a rare breed.

There isn't any man out there that holds all three of those qualities like him. They usually have one or two missing and trust me, with running a dating service with my five younger sisters—we've seen it all over the years.

Collectively we've witnessed enough disastrous dates to fill a whole season of bad reality TV, with guys and their towering lists of what they expect from a woman, such as looks to how well they can make a turkey sandwich.

I'm fairly sure if I ever threw Heath into our dating pool, he'd have a 100% match rate.

"You coming in, baby, or you gonna sit on that bike, looking sexy and cold all day?" His voice snaps me out of my thoughts.

Smiling, I look up to see Heath leaning against the doorframe of his home, one leg crossed in front of the other, while his arms are crossed over his broad chest. My heart flutters.

His hair is damp and wild from where he had clearly, just got out of the shower, his white t-shirt hugging his muscly, tattooed arms, and those grey sweatpants left nothing but exciting thoughts running crazy in my imagination. You know the saying ladies: *the way to a woman's heart is to feed her and wear grey sweatpants... because that dick print does wonders.*

Throwing my leg over the side of my bike, I trudge towards Heath, each step heavier than the last. My black army boots crunch against the snow, growing louder in my ears. My breath fogs in front of me as the cold claws at my skin, but it's nothing compared to the freezing knot twisting tighter in my chest.

His chestnut brown eyes rake over me, slow and deliberate. There's always something in that gaze—a hunger, a pull—that makes me feel like I'm being swallowed whole.

He always likes it when I wear my black leather jacket and ripped jeans. I see the smirk tugging at his lips, that knowing look as his arms open wide, waiting for me.

But something feels wrong. Too fast, too slow, like time itself is warping.

I take the last step, falling into his chest, my head tipping forward as his chin rests on it. His warmth surrounds me, but the longer I stay, the more it feels like I'm drowning. My arms tighten around him, desperate, scrunching his t-shirt in my fists like he might disappear if I let go. *Why does it feel like he's slipping away?*

"Welcome home, baby" he whispers, his voice smooth like honey. But instead of comfort, it sends a tremor through me, and tears well up, uninvited and sudden, blurring my vision. I'm shaking, but I don't know why. *Why am I shaking?*

I pull back to look at him, blinking through the haze of tears, expecting to see him–only he's not there when I do.

He's not here?

No. No. No. My hands are still raised, clutching at air, as my body falls forward, collapsing to where his chest should be. The weight of his absence crashes down like a punch, as my arms now circle my own stomach. His soothing embrace is gone; his warmth gone too. Leaving nothing but aching cold in its place.

The wind howls behind me, louder, hasher, slamming into me like it knows my world is unravelling. It screams into my ears, deafening. All I can hear is my own voice, silent but scared. *Why? Why is this happening?*

I don't understand, why is this happening?

"Heath," I call out as I search for him. "Heath!"

The hallway of his home slowly fades to black as I gasp loudly, desperately trying to catch my breath.

***

I bolt up into a seated position in bed. *It was just a dream.* Sweat pours from my forehead as I continue my mantra to myself. *It was just a dream. It was just another dream.*

"Did you die in here or something?" Annie, one of my younger sisters, deadpans as she waltzes through my bedroom like she owns the place.

"No, very much alive," I huff out, tossing the duvet off my sticky, sweaty body. My head flops back onto my pillow. "Just a bad dream," I mutter, mostly as reassurance for me rather than her.

"Seriously, it sounded like you were getting murdered in here. I was this close to calling the cops but then I got scared so I ran back to my room. Like, what if Heath was going to kill me, too?" she says, arms crossed, looking far too amused by her own panic.

My heart, which had just returned to its normal rhythm, decides to pick up at the mention of *his* name. *Shit, was I calling out to him in my sleep?*

Only one of my sisters really knows the whole story of Heath and I. And that's Brimley, and honestly, I only told her the depth of it because I was terrified she would make the same dumb mistake I did with Heath when it came to her and Shaun.

I didn't want her to ever question the *what ifs.* No regrets, type of thing. Thankfully, she heeded my advice and fixed the mess they were in.

If only I could fix my own mess.

My bed dips beside me as Annie comes into view from my poorly lit room. The concern for me is etched into her features.

"You look like dog poop, by the way." She smiles, wrapping her arm around my shoulders before carrying on, "Wanna talk?"

I shake my head from side to side, terrified that if I answer I might just open the floodgates of unshed tears I've locked up inside me, or worse; have to relive the day I watched him walk away. *For good.*

Chapter 2

Heath – 35 years old.

"Heeeeeath," my younger sister Marlee calls out to me, "Breakfast!"

She taps gently on my bedroom door three times. The action causes me to rub the side of my head to ease the inevitable migraine coming on. Although, my stomach does rumble at the mention of food. *Fuck, how did I get home?*

Last thing I remember was sitting at the bar, with Davy, my best friend, who was ordering another round of shots. *What a night, I guess?*

The empty whiskey bottle rattles along the hardwood floor as I stumble out of bed. My insides do somersaults as the murkiness thickens in my head.

On shaky legs, I make my way into my en-suite bathroom, turning the cold tap on and filling the sink up. I glance up and take in my reflection; the black bags sit heavy underneath my eyelids, my skin drawn and my hair an unkept mess.

I look like shit.

Scooping the icy water up in my hands, I splash my face with it, and even though I knew it was coming, I still jump at the sudden cold that freezes my skin.

After brushing my teeth and taking a quick shower, I head downstairs to join my sibling who is sitting at the kitchen table reading a book. *Another love story, I guess.* I pass her and pull open the fridge door.

Leaning against the kitchen counter, I brace myself for the retelling of how I ended up back in my childhood home and not the hotel I booked for the holidays, and of course, the lecture about drinking from Marlee.

Taking a swig from the orange juice bottle in my hand and letting out a deep breath, I sigh. "Okay, I'm ready. Hit me with it."

Marlee hums like she's contemplating the idea of talking to me before sighing loudly and turning another page in her book over.

Ten years younger than me, she still manages to be the more responsible one out of the two of us. She's a good kid. Shy until you know her, funny, and a little nerdy, but I love that about her. Marlee is the glue that holds me to my family.

I don't say that in a bad way. We are lucky to have two happily married parents, blessed to have a steady, stable home and upbringing, and neither of us have ever gone without our whole lives.

If I had it my way though, I would be travelling the world, every single day. Witnessing a new country or a new culture. Trying food I haven't tried before or drinking beverages you can't get in New York City.

I did it once before, five years ago; flew to Europe and spent a year moving from country to country. London to Paris to Spain to Italy. It was incredible and expensive, but worth it.

Like I said, Marlee ties me to the family, and on my travels, I had completely withdrawn from everyone, not answering a single call the entire year. A few texts here and there were sent to let them know I was still alive and a picture for proof, if Marlee was not satisfied with my response.

For a five-foot-two chick, my little sister really can scare the balls off a man. The telling-off she gave me when her and my parents came to pick me up from the airport was frightening. Safe to say, I will not be doing that again the next time I jump on a plane and visit the world.

She turns and faces me, her expression unreadable. Her brown hair swishes as she flicks one side of it over her shoulder sassily.

"Your fly is low." She points with her index finger towards my jeans, her lip curling up in disgust. "And your hair needs a serious intervention," she adds, before turning back around to her book on the table.

Pulling up the zipper on my pants, I move to sit beside her. "You know you can't stay mad like this all day, right?" I give her my best smile. "Tis the season, after all."

Slamming her book shut, she turns towards me, annoyance etched across her face. Huffing loudly, she whispers under her breath, "Cheese and rice."

I grin at her. That's her way of saying, *I'm pissed but I forgive you for being a moron.*

"Seriously, go get a haircut and, for the love of Santa, take a shower." She waves her hand as if she's trying to shoo me away. Turning back to her book, she cracks it open again.

Lifting my arm up in the air, I sniff my armpit dramatically. "I *did* take a shower." My voice comes out more whiny than I'd like. I sound like a petulant child than a fully grown man.

"Take another one!" she snaps, not even looking up. Realizing I've lost the battle, and not to wind her up further, I slink out of the kitchen and head back upstairs. Muttering under my breath, "*To shower again...or maybe bathe in holy water.*"

Closing my old bedroom door shut behind me, I make my way over to bed and begin the search for my phone. *Where the hell is it?*

Frantically checking my clothes from the night before, and even crawling halfway under the bed, I let out an exaggerated sigh.

"MARLEE, CALL MY PHONE, I CAN'T FIND IT!"

Moments later, my ringtone blares from across the room. I follow the noise, tripping over the whiskey bottle on the floor in my rush. The sound is coming from the dressing table where my phone vibrates furiously on top of a photo frame that's upside down.

"Found it!" I shout, picking it up with a triumphant grin.

As I grab the phone, I flip the photo frame back over. It's one of those old wooden frames, chipped and scratched from being shoved into various bags during my travels across Europe. Marlee always gives me crap about why I have a photo of a motorbike that's not even mine, framed like it's a precious artifact.

She knows it doesn't belong to me—the pink helmet hanging from the handlebar gives it away. I always tell her, "It's the one I'm going to buy one day."

Spoiler alert: I never will.

She is right about one thing, though. It's not my bike. It was Franny's. *My ex.* Yeah, I still have a framed photo of my ex's bike. *Totally normal, right?*

We had this grand plan of traveling Europe together. The whole *live our best lives* thing. Except when the time came, Franny decided she wanted to settle down, buy a house with a picket fence, maybe get a dog or a cat... or five cats. She wanted the quiet life. Me? I can barely handle the commitment of a Netflix subscription.

I know I'd make a great uncle someday—funny, slightly irresponsible, but still lovable. But a dad? Yeah, that's not happening.

Francesa and I parted ways on a 'see you soon' note. But the moment I got on that plane I knew that it was a lie we both told ourselves to make the goodbye hurt less.

As the plane lifted off, the weight of what we never said settled in. The 'what ifs' and the 'maybes' hung in the air, but I knew deep down, we were both heading for different paths *way before* we even packed our bags.

I guess having a picture of something that made me think of Franny on my travels reminded me of that last day with her and why we were never going to work. It wouldn't make sense to anyone, like my sister, but it made perfect sense to me.

Placing the picture facing back down on the dresser, I look down at my phone in my hand. Ten missed calls from Davy. *Shit, what happened?*

Hitting his caller ID on my phone, he picks up after a few rings.

"Yoooo maaaaan!" his voice drags down the receiver. Davy isn't into drugs, but his voice makes him sound like he's constantly got a joint in his hands.

"What's up? You called a bunch of times," I ask while putting him on loudspeaker and changing into my running shorts.

"I need a favor, a big one actually."

Rolling my eyes, I ask what kind of favor.

"Nana fell down the stairs last night. We gotta head to Florida to be with her." He pauses as his voice cracks.

Fuck, poor Dotty. "Shit, Davy. Is she okay?"

"We don't know yet, she's still in the hospital. So...with us gone, I kinda need some cover at work."

Davy works at a small bar in the suburbs of New York. It's usually quiet, except around this time of year when all the rich folks leave the city to retreat to their massive houses for Christmas. That's when Davy's bar gets extra busy.

"You know I got you covered. Send me your shift work and I'll sort it," I tell him confidently.

"I owe you, Heath. Thanks." He hangs up, not waiting for me to respond. I know he must be worried about his Nana. He'd have said goodbye otherwise.

Lacing up my trainers, I place my headphones over my ears. *Time to work off this hangover.*

Chapter 3

Francesca.

"Welcome to *Next Comes Love* dating services run by six sisters. Who, between us, have racked up enough failed relationships over the last decade to make you question why you are here in the first place. But hey, we are somehow convinced that we can help you find love this Christmas—how does that sound? Solid, right?" Lottie, the second youngest of us six, sarcastically snaps from across the table in our office.

"I dig it. Nothing says *holiday romance* like taking advice from people who have burned through more boyfriends than Christmas cookies," Annie adds, unbothered by the death stare she's receiving from Lottie, and how she just made us all sound slutty.

"Whatever, sign me up," I say.

Abby chimes in, "Count me in, too," backing up her twin, Annie.

Brimley lets out a long, dramatic sigh beside me. "Okay, first of all, change it to five failed sisters, because *hi*, I got Shaun, remember?" She raises an eyebrow. "And second, we've all been through the wringer when it comes to love, but that makes us pros at spotting red flags. We're basically mentors at this point. Call us the Yodas of Christmas matchmaking, just... you know, without the lightsabers."

"You know what we really need now?" We all turn towards our youngest sister Rory. She stares dreamily out the window, then spins around slowly in her chair, eyes glinting full of mischief with, no doubt, the best idea. Rory is our family's expert planner and prankster. "A Christmas slogan! Something fun... festive... and maybe a little naughty." She smirks.

The twins let out an exaggerated *Ooooh!* at the same time, and of course, they can't resist turning it into a competition of who can be the most inappropriate. *Same minds equal dirty sisters.*

"Santa's not the only one coming to town," Annie blurts out first, grinning.

"Be a *ho-ho-ho* this Christmas—*you* decide how you 'ho,'" Abby adds, complete with finger guns.

"Jingle his balls or jingle her bells—spread the cheer, either way!" Annie quips, earning a high five from her twin.

"Trim your tree, deck the halls, and... well, we will leave the rest up to you," Abby finishes with a wink.

Brimley claps her hands, practically bouncing in her seat. "Oh, I got one!" she shouts, beaming as she sing-songs, "Sleigh all day, play all night, bring the holiday spirit!" She's so proud it's almost adorable. We all burst out laughing, and I wrap my arms around her in a hug. But it doesn't last long, because the rest of the group boos her like she's just suggested cancelling Christmas. Her bottom lip sticks out in full pout mode, making the whole thing even funnier.

Zoning out to my sisters as they bounce ideas off each other, my mind wanders back to the nightmare I had last night. *They're getting worse and lasting longer.* I don't even realise I'm rubbing my temples until Brimley's voice cuts through my racing mind.

"You good?" she asks, giving me that sideways glance, one only a sister can give.

I blink, trying to shake the lingering unease from the dream. "Yeah, just... tired."

Brimley narrows her eyes at me. She's not buying it. She never does. "Tired? Or *dream* tired?"

I exhale, the tension in my chest tightening again. I should know better than to expect Annie to keep quiet. She's too much of a gossip for her own good.

"Nightmare," I admit quietly. "It's getting worse."

Brimley moves closer, lowering her voice so our other sisters can't hear. "Was it the same one?"

I nod. "Yeah... but this time it felt different. Like... like it was trying to tell me something."

Her eyes widen slightly, but she keeps her tone calm. "Heath again?"

"Yeah," I say, my voice a whisper. "He was right there, holding me, like he always did. But... then he was gone." My throat tightens, and I can feel the familiar ache of loss creeping in. "He keeps slipping away, Brim."

Brimley presses her lips into a thin line, her hand resting gently on my shoulder. "Maybe it's your mind trying to tell you something—something you haven't let yourself deal with yet."

I shake my head, the thought too overwhelming to process right now. "I thought I was over it. Over him."

She gives me a sympathetic smile. "You don't just get over someone like Heath. He was important to you."

Important. The word feels too simple, too light, for everything Heath was to me. He wasn't just important. He was… everything. And maybe that's why it still hurts. Maybe that's why he keeps showing up in my dreams, pulling me back into memories I've tried to bury.

"I just… I don't know how to make it stop," I say weakly.

Brimley squeezes my shoulder, her voice gentle but firm. "Maybe it's not about making it stop. Maybe it's about figuring it out. You're not alone in this, you know."

I nod, but my thoughts are already spiralling back to Heath. To the way he looked at me in the dream. To the way his presence felt so real, even though he's long gone from my life. It's like a ghost, haunting me in ways I never expected.

Brimley gives me one last look before turning back to the others, her expression thoughtful.

Chapter 4

Heath.

Christmas lights twinkle away, decorating the edge of the bar and a Christmas tree too tall for the room stood poorly ornamented and awkwardly in the corner. The low hum of conversation, mixed with the occasional clinking of glasses, and familiar Christmas songs play faintly in the background.

I wasn't supposed to work tonight, and when I say I wasn't supposed to work, I mean Davy wasn't, but Mike—the bar owner—called and explained that someone had called in sick and they needed an extra hand. *So, here I was.*

With my sleeves rolled up and wiping down the counter like it was second nature, I got right down to work. It's been a while since I could really say I've had a real job. I know it sounds bad—a 35-year-old man without a job. But hear me out: I was lucky, or got lucky, rather.

Right after I graduated college, I came up with a voice-to-text app. I'd been toying with the idea at least for a couple of years.

I'd gotten tired of having to write endless essays down on paper or typing them out.

There were plenty of competitors in the industry who had already created this type of app. So, yeah, my concept wasn't unique in any way, but mine had the edge that my rivals didn't... *I'd made it idiot proof.*

Simple, yet it worked. Long story short; I sold the idea to a wealthy businessman, and it set me up for life.

For a while, the idea of not working another day, ever, was appealing. Travelling helped fuel that freedom. But after a few years of that—it got boring.

Guess I can say it's nice to be working and not chilling in my apartment back in New Jersey... *alone*.

The place was busy, typical for a Friday night according to Mike, but it was manageable—enough to keep me occupied, and that's all I needed.

Just as I'm reaching for a bottle of whiskey, a girl barely old enough to be in here, comes up to the bar. She's leaning over just a little too far for comfort. Her lips painted red, and the look she giving me is the kind of look I've seen too many times before: playful, interested, and completely transparent.

"What can I get you?" I ask, keeping my tone polite but detached. I already know where this is heading, and I'm not in the mood to play along.

She gives me a slow smile, resting her elbows on the bar and leaning in closer, so her breasts push together. "How about you surprise me with your favorite?"

I feel one of my eyebrows raise, resisting the urge to roll my eyes. "You got a specific liquor in mind?"

She shrugged, biting her lip like she thinks it's cute. "I'll trust your judgment."

I turn, grabbing a bottle of vodka and mixing up something simple. All the while, I can feel her eyes on me, waiting for me to take the bait, to engage, to flirt back. But I ain't interested. Not tonight, not ever—not in the way she is hoping for.

I set the drink down in front of her. "Here you go."

She smiles, twirling the straw between her fingers. "You've got a good face, you know that? Bet you get a lot of attention working here."

I meet her gaze briefly, then go back to wiping down the bar. "I'm just here to make drinks."

Her smile falters for a second, clearly not the response she was expecting. "That's a shame. You seem like a guy who knows how to have a fun time."

I force a polite smile, nodding toward the other end of the bar. "If you need anything else, let me know."

The message is clear enough, and she picks up her drink, slipping back towards the table her and her friends were occupying.

Watching her go, I remind myself that I'm not here to be charmed or distracted. Complications like the one she was offering are not part of the favor Davy was needing, no matter how horny I am.

I'm here to help a friend in need... not to get laid. *Even if it has been months since I last fucked a woman.*

Chapter 5

Francesca

'Another day, another migraine.' I think to myself in frustration, as I stomp my way past groups of people.

Christmas shopping with my sisters is an experience, to say the least. Not the magical, holiday-movie kind of experience, where we stroll down twinkling, snow-dusted streets, sipping hot cocoa and laughing harmoniously.

Nope, it's more like a whirlwind of chaos, sarcasm, and trying to keep each other from impulse-buying every ridiculous, tacky decoration in sight.

But even though it's painful, I wouldn't trade it for anything. Well... maybe I would, but only on days when I forget how much I actually love them.

Today, it's just me and Brimley, the sister who has no concept of *just looking*.

We're at the mall, which is packed with desperate, last-minute shoppers who look like they'd rather be anywhere else. Brimley is practically bouncing with excitement, scanning every store window which seems to hold the key to Christmas joy.

"Ooooh, Fran, look!" She grabs my arm, pointing at a sparkly display in the window of a home décor store. There's a snowman pillow that looks like it's been doused in glitter, a wreath that could probably double as a disco ball, and a Santa figurine with a slightly unsettling grin.

"No," I say immediately, pulling her away before she can drag me into the glittery abyss. "We're not doing this again, Brim. Remember what happened with the reindeer?"

She grins, completely unbothered. "That was a one-time thing! And, okay, maybe it did get everywhere, but it was festive!"

"It was a glitter bomb," I deadpan. "Mom was finding sparkles in the kitchen six months later."

She shrugs, undeterred. "I thought it added character."

I roll my eyes, but I can't help smiling. Shopping with Brimley may be hazardous, but at least it's never boring.

We continue down the mall, dodging clusters of stressed-out parents and teenagers snapping selfies in front of the giant Christmas tree in the centre. Brimley chatters on about the upcoming holiday party we're hosting at the family business, and even though it's supposed to be about finding love, sometimes it feels more like a circus.

"Okay, so hear me out," Brimley says, leaning in to my side, like she's about to reveal some top-secret plan. "What if we had a holiday-themed speed dating event? Picture it: everyone in ugly Christmas sweaters, maybe a mistletoe station, and lots of Christmas cookies. It's festive, it's fun, and it's practically fool proof!"

I raise an eyebrow. "Fool proof? This is us we're talking about. Last time we did an event, Rory accidentally set off the sprinklers."

Brimley waves a hand, brushing off my scepticism. "That was an isolated incident. Besides, this is different! Christmas is romantic. People want to find love under the mistletoe. It's a Christmas cliché."

I sigh, pretending to think it over, but really, I know she's already sold me. Brimley has a way of making even the most ridiculous ideas sound plausible. And honestly, it does sound kind of cute.

"Fine, I'm in. But we're keeping Rory far, far away from any potential hazards. That means no lighters, no open flames, and absolutely no setting up a DJ booth."

"Deal!" She claps her hands, smiling.

We wander into a holiday gift shop, immediately assaulted by the overpowering scent of cinnamon and pine. Brimley makes a beeline for a rack of Christmas-themed pyjamas, holding up a pair covered in tiny elves and snowflakes.

"Fran, look! Matching pyjamas! We could get a set for all of us!"

I give her another sceptical look. "You want all six of us to wear matching pyjamas? Like some kind of overly enthusiastic Christmas cult?"

She gasps, clutching the pyjamas dramatically. "Yes! Think of the photo ops! We could make it our holiday card!"

I snort, shaking my head. "No way. I'm not getting roped into another one of your 'holiday traditions' that you just made up on the spot."

She pouts, giving me her best puppy-dog eyes, but I stand firm. There is no way I'm spending Christmas morning dressed like Cindy Lou Who's child.

After a while, we make our way to the food court, weighed down by an assortment of shopping bags. Brimley insists on buying a pretzel, and I grab a coffee, trying to shake off the weariness that's settled over me.

"You're awfully quiet today," Brimley asks, eyeing me with suspicion. "Everything okay?"

I shrug, not wanting to get into it. "Yeah, just tired."

She doesn't look convinced. "Didn't sleep well again?"

I smile wryly. "I don't know, Brim. The holidays are always so... overwhelming. Between work, family, and, well, everything else, it's like there's no time to just breathe."

She nods, surprisingly serious. "I get it. It's like we're supposed to be these magical holiday fairies, spreading joy and matchmaking couples, but sometimes I just want to curl up in bed and ignore the world."

"Exactly," I say, feeling a little lighter. Sometimes, just admitting it aloud helps. "But instead, here we are, planning Christmas-themed speed dating events and debating whether or not to buy a ten-foot inflatable Santa."

She laughs, rolling her eyes. "Well, that's the job, I guess. But hey, at least we're doing it together, right?"

I nod, smiling. "Yeah, that makes it a little better. I mean, who else would put up with our family's brand of chaos?"

Brimley grins, raising her pretzel in a mock toast. "To the chaos. And to surviving another holiday season without accidentally destroying the business."

I laugh, clinking my coffee cup against her pretzel. "I'll drink to that."

We sit there for a while, watching the crowds mill around the food court, people ladened with bags and kids hopped up on sugar, dragging their weary parents from one store to the next. It's a mess, but there's something comforting about it too. It's Christmas, after all. The season of togetherness, even if it is stressful.

After our little break, we head back into the fray, determined to finish our shopping. Brimley finds a set of ridiculously oversized Christmas ornaments, and I manage to talk her down from buying the complete set.

We bicker over whether we should get matching Christmas mugs—*I won that battle, thankfully*—and then we end up in front of a display of holiday-themed scented candles.

"Oh, this one's called Winter Wonderland!" Brimley says, holding up a candle that smells like peppermint. She inhales deeply, her eyes practically tearing up with joy. "It smells like Christmas in a jar!"

I wrinkle my nose, holding up a different candle labelled Fireside Glow.' It smells like cedarwood and a hint of smoke, warm and comforting. "This is way better. Smells like a real Christmas, not some candy-coated version."

She rolls her eyes, putting her candle back on the shelf. "You're such a holiday snob, Fran. Not everything has to be sophisticated."

"Hey, I just appreciate authenticity," I say, pretending to look offended.

She snorts, elbowing me playfully. "Okay, Miss Authenticity. Let's find something even you can't resist. Like maybe... oh! Ugly Christmas sweaters!"

I groan, but she's already dragging me toward a rack of sweaters that are so hideous, they almost come back around to being charming. There are sweaters covered in jingling bells, blinking lights, and garish patterns of reindeer and snowmen. Brimley holds up one with a giant, sequined Santa face and a caption that reads, "Sleigh All Day."

"Come on, Fran," she says, her eyes twinkling with mischief. "You know you want one."

"Absolutely not," I say firmly, crossing my arms. "There's a line, and this is it."

"Fine, suit yourself," she says, tossing the sweater over her arm. "But I'm wearing this to the Christmas party, and you'll regret not joining me."

I roll my eyes, but there's no point arguing. When Brimley gets an idea in her head, there's no stopping her. And honestly, a part of me is amused. Christmas wouldn't be the same without her outrageous ideas and her absolute refusal to take anything too seriously.

As we head toward the checkout line, Brimley starts brainstorming more ideas for our business's holiday marketing campaign.

"Okay, we do a countdown to Christmas, but each day we post a 'holiday dating tip' on our social media. Something festive, like 'Christmas gifts for new couples' or things like 'Find your perfect match before the clock strikes midnight on New Year'."

Chapter 6

Heath

The house smells like gingerbread, with hints of the apple cider Mom had left simmering on the stove before she ran out for her last-minute shopping spree.

Marlee and I have been left in charge of the Christmas tree—a task that sounded simple enough until you factored in my sister's obsession with *balance* and *aesthetic* and my tendency to hang ornaments in clumps to mess with her.

"Put that down," Marlee says sternly, without even looking at me as I pick up a hideous ornament—a reindeer with eyes that looked a little too... *intense* for the holidays.

I give her my best innocent look, raising my eyebrows. "This little guy? He's festive. Adds character."

Marlee turns, hand on her hip, her eyebrow raised. "Heath, I swear, if you put that thing on the tree, I'll take it down the second you turn your back."

"Grinch," I mutter, smirking as I set the reindeer back in the box.

It is always the same with Marlee; she has this way of keeping everything in line, even when she pretends to be laid-back.

Out of all of us, she is the one who keeps things balanced, keeps everyone grounded. And she does it in this way that makes you feel like she isn't doing anything at all, just... showing up, always when you need her most.

"So, are we going traditional this year?" I ask, picking up a string of red beads and draping it over my shoulder like a Christmas scarf.

Marlee rolls her eyes, but a smile tugs at her lips. "I was thinking more... classy, elegant. You know, an upmarket theme? Not the 'grab whatever looks weird' theme that you always go for."

"What's wrong with 'weird'?" I tease, tossing the beads to her. "Christmas is all about weird. I mean, look at Santa. The guy breaks into homes, eats everyone's cookies, and leaves presents in exchange. If that's not strange, I don't know what is."

Marlee snorts, catching the beads mid-air. "Okay, fair point. But maybe we can go for 'charmingly weird,' not 'looks-like-the-tree-fell-through-a-garage-sale weird'."

I can't argue with that, so I start unwrapping some ornaments, admiring the mix of old, fragile pieces we'd had since childhood and newer, shinier additions Mom had picked up over the years.

Each ornament has a story, a memory, and I find myself smiling as I pick up a small, ceramic star I'd made in elementary school. The edges are lopsided, and my name is scrawled across the back in what I could only describe as serial-killer handwriting, but it's perfect.

Marlee eyes it with a grin. "That one's... unique."

"Hey," I say, holding it up proudly, "This star has survived more Christmases than you have. Respect the legacy."

She laughs, reaching out to take it from me. "Fine, fine. It can go… on the back of the tree."

"Rude," I mutter, though I'm smiling.

Decorating with Marlee always has this comforting, familiar rhythm to it—she sets things in place, and I inevitably fuck with them, trying to get a reaction out of her. It was like a tradition at this point, one of the few things that hadn't changed.

We work in silence for a while, hanging ornaments and stringing lights, each lost in our own thoughts. Marlee hums along to the Christmas music playing softly in the background, her movements precise as she arranges the decorations just so.

I can see how carefully she works, how every placement matters to her, and it struck me just how much Marlee always cares about the details. About making things right, even when nobody else notices.

She's always been this way and it's a lot to put on someone, especially someone younger than me. Sometimes, I worry about that—about whether she felt like she had to be the responsible one because I… well, because I wasn't always around.

"So," she says after a while, breaking the silence, "How's everything going with you?"

I shrug, keeping my focus on the string of lights I was untangling. "Fine, I guess. Just… you know." I trail off; truth is, other than drinking I haven't really got much on.

Marlee gives me a look, and I can practically feel her eyes boring into the side of my head. "That's vague. Try again."

I sigh, not really wanting to get into it. But whether I like it or not, Marlee has a way of getting the truth out of me. "Things have been… a little rough," I admit. "I'm fine, but… everything else just feels kind of off, you know? Like I need to be doing something, but what that something is, I don't know."

She nods, her expression softening as she hangs a delicate glass ornament on a branch. "I get it. Sometimes, it feels like everyone else has it all figured out, and you're just... floating."

I laugh, though it comes out more bitter than I intended. "Yeah. Floating. Or maybe sinking, depending on the day."

Marlee pauses, looking over at me with that serious, thoughtful expression she gets sometimes. "Heath, you know it's okay to feel lost, right? You don't have to have it all together and you don't have to pretend with me."

I swallow, the weight of her words hitting me harder than I'd expected. "It's just... hard, you know? It feels like everyone's moving forward, doing big things, and I'm... here. In the same place."

She doesn't say anything for a moment, just reaches over and places a hand on my arm, her touch warm and reassuring. "Heath, you've done more than you realize. And even if you feel stuck, it doesn't mean you aren't moving forward. Sometimes, the progress is just... quieter."

I nod, feeling a lump form in my throat. I hate feeling like this, like I am somehow disappointing her or letting her down. But she doesn't look disappointed. She just looks... worried.

"Anyway," I say, clearing my throat and forcing a smile, "Enough about me. Let's focus on this masterpiece of a tree."

She rolls her eyes but smiles back, reaching for another ornament. "Fine. But you're still letting me pick the theme."

Chapter 7

Francesca

It's Christmas Eve, and all afternoon my sisters have been laughing, singing carols, and wrapping last-minute gifts with Mom and Dad. Our childhood home is full of warmth, full of joy, but all day today, I found it hard to breathe.

The walls felt too close, the laughter too loud. My chest tightened, and I couldn't shake the feeling that the room was closing in on me.

Not again.

My heart raced, pounding against my ribs like it was desperate to escape. My vision blurred, and my breaths came in shallow gasps. I needed to get out. I needed air.

Before anyone could notice, I slipped out the door, my fingers trembling as I fumbled for my pink helmet.

The frosty night air hit my face, sharp and biting, but it wasn't enough to calm the panic raising in my chest. My hands shook as I pulled on my helmet and swung a leg over my bike. *I just needed to ride. To escape.*

Speeding down the road, the roar of the engine and the chilly wind cut through my thoughts, but the tightness in my chest stayed with me. I pushed the throttle harder, the quiet streets flashing by as Christmas lights blurred in the distance.

The night was eerily still—too still—but my mind was anything but.

Heath's face, his voice, the way he used to calm me down, kept flashing through my head, but he wasn't here. He hadn't been for a long time.

Halfway down a quiet lane, the bike sputters. "No, no, no," I cry out, my voice shaky, as I try to push it further, but the engine coughs, sputters again, and dies. Pulling into the side of the road, the sudden silence is deafening.

I rip off my helmet, gasping for air as the panic swells inside me again, harder this time. My breath comes in ragged bursts, my hands trembling uncontrollably. *What now?* Alone. I'm completely alone.

The lane stretches out in front of me, no cars, no lights, and since I left the house just as my panic attack kicked in, I didn't think to pick up my phone. A sob breaks free. It's just me and the soft glow of distant stars out here.

I try to focus, to steady my breath, as my heart pounds louder and louder in my ears. My thoughts keep racing—*Heath*. If only he were here. He'd know what to say. He'd know how to make this all go away, how to steady me and keep me grounded.

I sink down next to my bike, my hands burying themselves in my hair as I try to control the next sob that's claws its way up my throat. The quiet is too loud. The loneliness is too real. I need him. I need something to make this stop.

But he isn't coming.

And I don't know if I can do this on my own.

The wintry night bites as I sit next to my bike, frozen in more ways than one. I stare down the empty track, feeling the first flakes of snow begin to fall, delicate and soft at first, but soon the air is thick with them, each flake landing cold and sharp against my skin.

I can't stay here. Not in the middle of nowhere, with the snow coming down harder by the minute and my breath clouding in front of me. I use what adrenaline I have surging through my veins and push forward.

Gripping the handlebars of my bike, I force my legs to start moving, pushing the dead weight of the motorcycle down the road.

Except for the sound of snow crunching beneath my boots and the occasional scrape of the bike's tires against the ground, the world around me is silent.

I don't know how long I pushed before I saw the faint glow of lights up ahead. A bar—small, tucked away, and somehow exactly what I need. Relief washes over me as I stumble toward it, hoping for warmth, for a phone, for anything that would get me out of this ordeal.

Pushing on the wooden door, it creaks open, and I step inside, the warm air hitting me like a slap in the face after the freezing cold. I don't even stop to take in the Christmas lights strung across the ceiling or the soft babble of conversation. I am too focused on catching my breath, shaking off the snow that clings to my clothes. The smell of wood burning, alcohol, and something fried fills the air, reminding me of how far I'd come from the world of holiday cheer.

That's when I see him.

Standing behind the bar, wiping down a glass with a rag like he had done it a thousand times. *Heath.*

My heart stops, completely frozen for what feels like a lifetime.

The panic I'd been running from twists into something sharper. I blinked, certain I'm seeing things. *It can't be him. Not here.* Not in this tiny bar in the middle of nowhere, on Christmas Eve, of all nights.

But it is him.

Heath.

His hand halts on the glass, his gaze locking onto mine. Heath's expression shifts from confusion to disbelief, just as mine probably did. He stands perfectly still, the noise of the bar fading into the background as if the world tilted on its axis and left only the two of us standing in this moment.

I felt the air rush out of my lungs, and for a second, I forgot about everything else—about the broken bike, the blizzard, the panic that had driven me here. All I can see is Heath, his eyes wide, his jaw clenched as he's trying to figure out if I am real.

Neither of us say a word. We just stare at each other, stuck in place, the weight of everything that happened between us pressing down like the snow piling up outside.

Chapter 8

Heath

The bar door opened, and a gust of freezing air swept in, along with a figure bundled up against the snow. I didn't think much of it at first. Another stranded traveller, maybe, or a local who'd had too much Christmas cheer and needed one last drink to warm up. But then I looked up, and my heart stopped.

Franny.

For a second, my little Pixie completes me again.

No, fuck her!

But the shock hits me so hard, I can't move. She stands there just inside the doorway, snow clinging to her hair and her coat, her cheeks flushed from the cold. She hasn't even seen me yet—she is too busy shaking off the snow, catching her breath as she takes in the warmth of the bar.

I stay frozen; my hand clenching around the glass I'd been cleaning.

Part of me wants to bolt, to disappear into the back room and pretend she hadn't just walked into my life again after all this time. But my feet stay rooted to the spot, like I'm waiting for something.

Finally, she looks up, and our eyes meet. I see the moment she recognizes me—the way her expression shifts from relief to pure, stunned disbelief. She doesn't say anything, and neither do I.

We just stare at each other, both caught in the past, in everything that was left unfinished between us.

"What are you doing here, Francesca?" I manage; my voice rougher than I intended. It's like I have to remind myself to breathe, to keep my hands steady.

She blinks, as if she's forgotten how to answer a simple question. "My bike..." She gestures vaguely toward the door. "It broke down a few miles back. No help's coming tonight—it's Christmas Eve, and everything's closed. So, I was just looking for somewhere to wait out the storm."

Of course, she ended up here. I swallow the bitterness that rose in my throat and force myself to nod. "You can stay here until the storm lets up," I say, keeping my tone as neutral as possible. "There's a room in the back if it gets too late."

She mutters a quiet thanks and takes a seat at the bar, her hands shaking as she clasps them together. I notice it, of course—just like I notice the tiredness in her eyes and the way her shoulders slump, like she's been carrying something heavy for a long time. But I won't give in to that old instinct to comfort her. Not now.

Without a word, I grab a bottle from the shelf and pour her a drink. Whiskey, the way she used to like it. The glass clinks softly as I slide it toward her, and she looks up, a flicker of surprise crossing her face.

"Here," I say, already turning away to busy myself with the bar. "It'll help with the cold."

Feeling her eyes on me as she sips the drink, I feel the questions she is holding back.

The tension in the air between us is thick and heavy, like we're both balancing on a thin sheet of ice. I want to break the silence, to demand to know why she'd come here of all places, why she couldn't just stay out of my life, like I'd thought she would after everything that happened. But I keep my mouth shut, my jaw clenched tight, as I fight to hold back the war brewing inside me.

Finally, she speaks, her voice soft, silky, hesitant. "Why are you here, Heath? In this town, I mean. It's so far from…"

"From everything?" I finish for her, a bitter smile tugging at my lips. "Yeah. That was kind of the point."

She flinches, and I see a flash of guilt in her eyes, but I don't let myself feel sorry for her. Not after *she* made that choice—choosing comfort, stability, over what we could've had together. *I loved her, for fucks sake.*

She opens her mouth to respond, but I shake my head, cutting her off. "Don't. Don't come in here with your questions, looking for answers. You made your choice, Pixie. You stayed."

The words hang heavy in the air, and I can see the pain they cause her, but I don't take them back. I can't, not yet, at least.

"I'm sorry," she whispers, her voice cracking, and I can see her fighting back tears. "I thought… I thought I was doing what was best for both of us."

A harsh laugh escapes me before I can stop it. "Best? Is that what you call this?"

She looks down, her face pale, and I almost regret the roughness in my tone. Almost. But the wound is still too raw, too deep for apologies to mend.

"Maybe we weren't right for each other," she says, only just loud enough to hear, but the words still hit me like a punch to the gut. "Maybe we would've just ended up hurting each other even more."

For a moment, I feel something ease inside me, the faint memory of all the nights we'd spent together, dreaming about the future, about the places we'd go and the life we'd build. But just as quickly, I shove the memories down, locking them away behind the walls I built to keep her out.

"Yeah, maybe," I mutter, pouring myself a drink and avoiding her gaze. "Or maybe you were just too scared to face what you really wanted."

The silence returns, thick and suffocating. She doesn't argue, doesn't try to defend herself, and I wonder if she finally realizes the truth I've known all along—that she's always been more comfortable staying put. She wanted me, but only if I was willing to stay in her world, to settle for less than what I'd dreamed of. And I couldn't do it, not then and not now.

I take a long sip of my drink, letting the warmth burn away some of the cold that has settled inside me. I can feel her watching me, can sense the regret in her eyes, but I don't let myself soften. Not this time.

"I'm sorry," she says again, barely a whisper. "For not fighting harder."

I look at her, and I want to believe in second chances. But the years of loneliness, and the nights spent with nothing but the memory of her to keep me company start to creep in. I shake my head, a sad smile tugging at the corners of my mouth.

"Some things can't be fixed, Francesca," I say quietly. "Not even by an apology."

The finality of it settles over us, and I watch the hope drain from her face, replaced by a sadness that mirrors my own. We both made choices, both walked away, and now there is nothing left.

She drains her glass, her movements slow and defeated, and I know this is the end. The real end this time. She stands, her voice a murmur. "Goodbye, Heath."

I don't respond, don't even look up as she walks toward the door. The sound of her footsteps fade, and I keep my eyes fixed on the bar, my grip tight around the glass as if it is the only thing anchoring me in this moment.

When she is gone, I allow myself a glance out the frosted window, catching a glimpse of her retreating figure, small and fragile against the endless white of the snowstorm. I wonder if she'll make it through the night, if she'll ever think back on this moment, on what we had and what we'd thrown away.

As the snow continued to fall, blanketing the world in silence, I can't shake the feeling that some stories aren't meant to end this way.

Our story isn't meant to end this way..

Chapter 9

Francesca.

The snow fell in thick, unrelenting sheets, as I wade through the darkness, yet I keep going, one step after another, clutching the handlebars of my broken bike.

Just keep going. Don't look back.

I know it was foolish, the weight of being around him—especially tonight, of all nights.

Still, I need to get away, to escape the ache that seeing him brought up, the memories of us that cling to me like a second skin.

The bar had been warm and comforting, but the air between Heath and me had grown colder with his every word. His eyes, still familiar and intense, had held a glint of resentment. We'd both made choices, I get it, *though* I'd stupidly thought, we were okay with that.

Glancing down at my bike—no help is coming tonight; this town had shut down early by the looks of it. And any garage or repair shop would be locked up tight until the day after tomorrow.

I just hope I can make it back home, on foot, the distance feels longer, more daunting now that I can't see the road ahead.

Shaking my head from side to side. I let out a scream, *Pull yourself together, Francesca. You can do this!*

"Francesca!"

The sound of my name cuts through the quiet night, startling me. I freeze, my heart pounding as I turn to see a figure approaching through the haze of snow. I don't need to see his face to know it's him—Heath—coming after me just like he used to, back when I thought he was someone I could depend on.

He stops a few feet away, breathing hard, his hair dusted with flakes and his jaw clenched tight. "What the hell do you think you're doing?" he asks, his voice harsh but layered with something else—concern, maybe, or frustration. I can't tell.

"I'm going home," I reply, trying to keep my voice steady, unaffected. But the truth is, I'm exhausted, and his sudden appearance has thrown me off balance.

"It's snowing too hard, Francesca," he says, taking a step closer. "You can't walk home in this."

I grip the handlebars tighter, looking down at the bike as if it will somehow solve this whole mess for me. "I'm fine. I'll manage."

Heath lets out a frustrated groan, running a hand through his hair. "This is ridiculous," he mutters. "You're going to get yourself hurt out here. Come back to the bar. Wait out the storm, and in the morning, I'll help you get your bike fixed."

I want to argue, to tell him I don't need his help, that I am perfectly capable of handling this on my own. But the cold is seeping into my bones, and the snow is coming down harder, making a wall between me and the safety of my home.

He is right, and I know it, but admitting that feels like another kind of defeat.

"I can't go back there," I say quietly, my voice barely audible above the wind. "I can't just... pretend everything's okay. Not after..."

My words trail off and I swallow hard, refusing to look at him. The memories of our last days together flicker in my mind—intense arguments, broken promises, the plans we'd made and abandoned. He had wanted me to leave with him, to take on the world together, and I'd been too afraid to step outside the boundaries of the life I'd known. That choice had driven a wedge between us.

"Francesca," he says, lighter this time, almost a plea. "I'm not asking you to pretend. Just... don't be reckless. Please."

I look up at him, his face partially hidden in the shadows cast by the streetlight. There is an openness in his expression, something vulnerable that I hadn't seen in years. It strikes me, making me hesitate. Maybe he's changed, or maybe I've changed. *I'm not sure anymore.*

"Why do you care?" I ask, the question slipping out before I can stop it.

Heath's eyes meet mine, steady and unflinching. "Because I still care about you, Francesca. Even if everything's different now. I don't want to see you get hurt."

A lump forms in my throat, and I feel the sting of tears welling up, but I push them back. I don't want him to see me like this, don't want him to think I am still holding onto something we'd both let go of a long time ago.

"It's just a few miles," I argue weakly, even though I can't feel my toes.

He sighs again, this time with more resolve, and steps closer, close enough that I can see the flecks of snow on his eyelashes. "Please, Francesca. Don't be stubborn just to prove a point. Come back. I don't want you out here alone."

I hesitate, torn between my pride and the truth staring me in the face. The storm is worsening, and the way back is treacherous. I glance down the road, the path home hidden behind a veil of white, and then back at him. For all my resistance, there is a part of me that wants to give in, to let him take care of me, just this once.

"Fine," I say, my voice a whisper. "Just until the storm passes."

Heath nods in relief and reaches out, taking my broken bike from my hands, his fingers brushing mine for the briefest moment. It is such a small gesture, but it sends a shiver through me that has nothing to do with the cold. I draw my hand back quickly, not wanting him to notice.

The walk back to the bar is silent, our footsteps crunching in the snow and the distant howl of the wind. He walks close beside me, his presence solid and steady, and for the first time in a long time, I feel a strange sense of comfort. I've been alone for so long, and have pushed so many people away, including him. But tonight, in the thick of the storm, having someone beside me feels like a relief I didn't realize I needed.

When we reach the bar, he holds the door open for me as I step in. I feel the tension start to melt from my shoulders as the heat from the fire wraps around me. Heath follows, closing the door against the storm, and sets the bike aside.

"Sit down," he says gruffly, gesturing toward the booth nearest the fireplace. "You're shivering."

I resist the urge to snap back, to tell him I don't need his pity, but the exhaustion is starting to weigh on me, and I am too tired to fight.

I take a seat, holding my hands out toward the fire, letting the warmth seep into my frozen fingers.

He disappears behind the bar, and I hear the sound of him moving around, pouring drinks, the clink of glasses and bottles. He returns with a steaming mug and sets it down in front of me. Hot chocolate, with a splash of whiskey, just like he used to make on nights when we'd stay up late, talking about the dreams we'd never quite reached.

"Thank you," I murmur, wrapping my hands around the mug, feeling the warmth spread through my palms.

Heath takes a seat across from me, watching me quietly, and I feel the weight of his gaze, heavy with things left unsaid. I'm not sure if either of us are ready to talk, to dig up the past that lies buried between us, but the silence stretches on, making it impossible to ignore.

"I'm sorry," he says finally, his voice low, almost hesitant. "For the way things ended. I should've handled it differently."

Unable to meet his eyes, my voice is a whisper when I answer, "I'm sorry, too. I know I hurt you, I just wasn't ready. I was scared."

He nods, and for a moment, there is a flicker of understanding in his eyes. "I get it. I was just as scared."

I've spent so long building walls around myself, trying to forget, but sitting here with him, those walls are starting to crumble.

We don't say much after that. We just sit together, sharing the silence, watching the snowfall outside. And for a little while, it is enough.

Chapter 10

Heath.

The storm howls outside, piling snow against the windows, making it clear that nobody else will be coming in tonight. The has bar is quiet except for the occasional pop from the fire and the faint hum of the old radio by the counter, tuned to a holiday station.

I glance across the room at Francesca, still curled up in the corner booth by the fireplace, her hands wrapped around a mug of hot chocolate. She is looking down at the cup, completely lost in thought, and for the first time in what feels like years, I don't feel the bitterness rise up at the sight of her.

It is strange having her here. After all the ways we'd hurt each other, after all the years that had passed, I thought we were better off keeping our distance. Yet here she is, stranded by the storm on Christmas Eve, her bike broken and her pride too fierce to admit she might need a little help. *Typical Pixie.* I try to pretend I'm not glad she is here, but I've always been terrible at lying to myself.

As if sensing my gaze, she looks up, catching my eyes. There is a flicker of something soft and almost shy in her expression, a side of her I've missed. The silence is comfortable, and I find myself savouring it, letting it stretch between us without the pressure to fill it with words.

Then, the radio crackles, and a familiar song came on—one of those old Christmas tunes that has been around forever. The kind that can make you feel a little warmer inside, no matter what is going on. Glancing back over at her, she had a faint smile on her face, her fingers tapping along to the beat on her now empty mug.

I don't know what comes over me. Maybe it is the warmth of the fire, the softness in her smile, the need to comfort her or just the nostalgia of an old song playing on Christmas Eve in an empty bar. Before I can second-guess myself, I walk over to her booth and hold out my hand.

"Dance with me?" I ask, trying to sound casual, like this isn't the most impulsive, ridiculous thing I've done in years.

She raises an eyebrow, her eyes darting from my hand to my face, searching for any hint that I am joking. "Dance?" she repeats, the scepticism clear in her voice. "In this empty bar? To a Christmas song?"

I shrug, trying to keep my tone light, though my heart is beating a little faster than I'd like to admit. "Why not? It's just us here. Besides, you owe me one. I saved you from that blizzard out there, remember?"

She lets out a laugh, shaking her head, but there is warmth in her eyes, like she is remembering the better times, too. She glances at my hand, hesitating, and for a moment, I think she might brush me off. But then, slowly, she sets down her mug and slips her hand into mine.

Her fingers are warm, and a little spark shoots through me at the touch. I pull her up, and we move toward the middle of the bar where there is just enough space to pretend it's a dance floor.

She's close now, close enough that I can see the faint dusting of freckles on her nose, the way her cheeks are still flushed from the cold. I haven't been this close to her in years, and it feels… amazing. Like slipping into an old coat that still fits perfectly.

"You know, I don't remember you being much of a dancer," she teases, a mischievous smile playing at her lips.

"That's because I'm not," I admit, grinning. "But maybe you'll notice more if I keep stepping on your feet."

"Oh, I've already noticed," she says, laughing.

I chuckle, pulling her a little closer as the music swells around us. We move slowly, swaying more than dancing, really, but neither of us seem to care. The song is soft and sweet, and the whole room feels wrapped up in it, like the warmth from the fire is mixing with the melody, melting away the years of distance between us.

"Do you remember that time we tried to dance at the summer festival?" I ask, grinning at the memory.

She groans, rolling her eyes. "How could I forget? You spun me around so fast I nearly took out the punch bowl."

"And you still haven't forgiven me for it," I reply, feigning a wounded look.

"Oh, I forgave you…eventually," she says, winking then smiling up at me.

I chuckle, shaking my head.

We sway in silence for a while, just listening to the music, the lyrics about love and Christmas. It feels surreal, holding her like this after all the hurt we'd caused each other. But the more I look at her, the more I feel the old feelings stirring up—the easiness, the comfort, the part of me that has never really stopped caring about her, no matter how hard I've tried to convince myself otherwise.

I'm still thinking about it, about the strangeness of this whole night, when she looks up at me with that half-smile. "You know, this isn't exactly how I imagined spending my Christmas Eve," she says, a hint of amusement in her tone.

"Yeah?" I ask, raising an eyebrow. "How'd you imagine it?"

She shrugs, glancing away for a moment, her cheeks turning a little red. "Not trudging through a snowstorm with a broken bike, that's for sure."

I chuckle. "Well, if it makes you feel any better, I wasn't expecting to be rescuing you from the side of the road tonight, either."

She rolls her eyes, but there is something almost... vulnerable in her gaze. "Guess neither of us ended up where we thought we would," she murmurs.

I nod, my hand resting on the small of her back, feeling the warmth of her through the fabric of her sweater. "Yeah. But I'm starting to think that's okay."

We keep swaying, the song carrying us along, and before I realize it, I'm humming along, the melody pulling me in. Francesca looks up at me, a glimmer of surprise in her eyes.

"You're singing?" she asks, a teasing lilt in her voice.

I shrug, trying to play it off. "Well, desperate times, right?"

She laughs, and it feels like we are back in time, just two people dancing without a care in the world. She leans her head against my shoulder, her hair brushing against my cheek, and I let myself breathe her in, the faint smell of vanilla that is so unmistakably her.

"You're not so bad at this," she murmurs, her voice soft.

"Don't sound so surprised," I shoot back, smirking. "You're not giving me enough credit."

She pulls back just enough to meet my eyes, her smile fading into something softer, more serious. "Heath... do you think..." She hesitates, her gaze dropping to the space between us. "Do you think it's possible to just... start over?"

I don't answer right away, her question settling over me. I think about all the years of anger and resentment, all the times I'd told myself I was over her, that we were better off apart. But standing here, with her in my arms, the soft strains of a Christmas song filling the room, I realize something I've been too stubborn to admit.

I've fucking missed her, so much.

"Maybe," I say quietly, my hand moving to brush a stray strand of hair behind her ear. "Maybe we could try."

She looks up at me, her eyes bright with something I can't quite place, and in that moment, I feel a surge of hope, fragile and new, but *real*. Leaving only the possibility of what we might still find.

The song comes to an end, but neither of us move. We stand there in silence and for the first time in a long time, I feel like I am exactly where I am supposed to be.

"Happy Christmas, Pixie."

She smiles, her fingers tightening in mine. "Happy Christmas, Heath."

Chapter 11

Francesca.

The warmth of the fire seeps into my skin as I stay in Heath's arms, my head resting against his shoulder. The Christmas song plays on the old radio, filling the empty bar with a comforting melody.

It is surreal being here, dancing with him in the middle of a storm, on Christmas Eve of all nights. It's the kind of moment I'd once dreamed about, back when things were simpler, when I still believed that love could conquer anything. But life has a way of getting complicated, and our love was one of the casualties.

Catching his gaze. His eyes are steady, with a glimmer of something that sends a shiver down my spine. The connection that had once bound us together—it's still here, It's just been buried under years of misunderstanding.

A small laugh escapes me, and he raises an eyebrow. "What's so funny?"

Feeling a blush creep up my cheeks. "This... all of this. It feels like something out of a movie."

Heath chuckles; a low, deep sound that makes my heart skip a beat. "Well, if it's a movie, we're definitely the tragic leads," he says, half-smiling. "You know, the ones who keep messing up their timing."

I laugh again, but there's a bittersweet edge to it, this time. He isn't wrong; timing has never been our strong suit. We've always had this undeniable connection but life has a way of pulling people in different directions.

The song changes to something slower, softer, and I feel his grip on me tighten ever so slightly. My heart pounds as I meet his gaze again, my breath catching in my throat at the intensity in his eyes. His hand is warm against my waist, his thumb brushing lightly over the fabric of my sweater, sending a thrill through me that I can't ignore.

He chuckles deeply at my blushing, his fingers tracing small circles against my back, a touch so subtle yet so electrifying that I feel my skin heat up. I should pull away, remind myself of all the reasons this is a bad idea. If we're starting over, we should go slow. But the truth is, my heart didn't want to. *Not tonight.*

He leans in a little closer, and I feel my pulse quicken, a need of want spreading through me. His gaze drops to my lips. "Francesca..." His voice is a low, rough whisper.

"Yeah?" I reply, my own voice trembling.

He hesitates, his gaze searching my face as if looking for some kind of permission. And then, before I can think, before I can talk myself out of it, I lean forward, closing the distance between us.

The kiss is gentle at first, tentative, but then his hand moves up to cradle my face, his fingers brush my cheek, and I feel a heat bloom inside me, spreading through every nerve in my body. Like all the years of restraint, all the hurt and longing, pour out in this single moment.

His lips move against mine, slow then deeper, hungrier. My hands find their way to his shoulders, and I feel his muscles tense beneath my touch, solid and real, grounding me in a way that feels dangerously addictive.

I pull back for a moment, gasping for air, my mind racing, my heart pounding as I look up at him. His eyes are dark, intense, filled with a desire that I haven't seen in years. A shiver runs down my spine.

"Are you… is this what you want?" he asks, his voice dark, his gaze steady and unyielding. "Because I don't want to do this if it's just the storm, or the song, or—"

I silence him with another kiss, my hands slipping up to tangle in his hair. I don't want to talk, don't want to dissect this, or weigh the consequences. All I know is that I want him, need him, and for the first time in a long time, I don't want to think about tomorrow.

He groans against my lips, his arms wrapping around me, pulling me closer, and I melt into him, my body fitting against his as if we've never been apart. His hands move to my waist, sliding beneath my sweater, painfully slow as he rolls it up my body and over my head.

I can feel his heartbeat against mine as I tug his shirt over his head. His mouth instantly moves down to my jaw, trailing kisses along my neck, each one leaving a trail of heat in its wake. I tilt my head back, my breath hitching, my fingers tightening in his hair as I feel myself falling, slipping into a world where only he exists.

The music, the warmth of the fire, the weight of his hands on my skin—it is all too much, too perfect, and I know I am in trouble.

Chapter 12

Heath.

Outside, the snow continues to fall, thick and hard, burying outside of the bar building in white.

Looking down at Franny, her eyes met mine. She looks up at me with that fire that has always driven me crazy.

There is so much I want to say, so many things I want to make right. But instead, I find myself leaning in, my hand reaching to gently tuck a strand of hair behind her ear.

"Francesca," I speak quietly.

I feel her lean into me, her hand sliding up to rest on my chest, and that spark turns into something deeper, something I can't ignore.

The kiss deepens, a intense pull that seems to unravel us. I feel her fingers curl around my shoulders, her nails digging in, pulling me closer, and I can't help the small groan that escapes me.

My hand moves up, cupping her face, my thumb brushing her cheek as I kiss her with everything I have, every unsaid word and unresolved feeling.

She pulls back slightly, just enough to look up at me, her breathing uneven, her cheeks flushed.

"Are you okay with this?" she whispers.

In response, I lean down, pressing a light kiss to her forehead, then her temple, then her cheek. "I've never been more sure about anything, in my life." My lips brush against her skin, feeling her shiver under my touch.

She pulls me back down, crushing her lips on mine with a fierce urgency that catches me off guard but lures me under, deeper and deeper. My hand moves to her waist, tugging her closer, feeling the heat radiating between us, a pull that feels magnetic, irresistible.

I back us up slowly, guiding her toward the corner booth where she'd been sitting earlier, and as her legs hit the edge of the seat, she lets out a giggle, breathless and warm, sending a rush of warmth to my dick—one that I haven't felt in years.

Smiling back, I rest my forehead against hers for a moment, to catch my breath. I feel the electric charge between us that seems to hum louder with every heartbeat.

My hands slide to her waist, lifting her gently onto the booth seat, bringing her to my level as our kisses grow deeper and more fevered. She leans back slightly, pulling me down with her, her eyes dark and unreadable, filled with a heat that I can't resist.

I find myself pressing gentle kisses across her exposed breasts, trailing them down towards where her jeans sit tightly on her hips. Feeling her pulse quicken beneath my lips, I rush to undo her button and pull down her zipper. She tilts her head back, a breathless sigh escaping her lips, and it takes everything in me to keep my touch gentle.

"Francesca," I whisper, my voice unrecognisable.

"Don't stop," she whines, and it undoes me.

Tugging her jeans down towards her army boots, I hurriedly undo the shoes and pull them off along with her pants. I kiss my way back up towards her soaking pussy. My fingers slide up and down her clit, teasing her, before my resolve snaps completely and my face buries itself between her legs.

My own groan catches me off guard as it rumbles through my chest at the taste of her. So, fucking sweet, just like I remembered.

"My favourite fucking meal."

"Jesus, Heath!" she cries out, grabbing the back of my head, forcing my face further into her as she grinds her cunt against my face. She chases her high until she cries out once more and her juices fill my mouth.

Wiping across my mouth, a smile creeping across it as I rise from my knees, I pull my pants down to release my hard and straining dick from them. I look down at my Pixie, dazed and settled, her legs wide open, ready for me to fuck her...ready for me to remind her of all she's missed over the years.

"I don't plan on making love to you tonight princess," I tease, while moving my hand up and down my cock.

She raises a brow at me in a challenge. "Good, I was hoping for that."

Licking her lips, her eyes wild and hungry, she stretches out her arms to me, wanting to pull me in and, no doubt, inside her. I wipe the precum off the end of my shaft with my finger, holding it out to her. Wasting no time, she pulls herself forward, moaning as her lips wrap around my finger and suck off my cum. *Music to my ears.*

Grabbing a condom from my wallet and ripping it open, I roll it down my dick, ordering Francesca to lay on top of our clothes on the floor in front of the fire.

I move between her legs, gently kissing along her jaw as I slowly inch my way inside her. She hisses in pain, and I stop to allow her to adjust to me again, before fully settling inside her. Grabbing my cheeks, she nods up at me, giving me permission to move.

Like an addict who's gone without his fix for too long, I pull back and slam into her, over and over, sprinting after the pressure of pleasure building inside me. She moans like a fan girl cheering me on. Our mouths clash against one another, my fingers digging into her hips like an anchor, as she sucks on the side of my neck.

"Heath, fuck. Heath, I'm so-" Her words cut off as her pussy tightens around my cock, before she's crying out in ecstasy.

I feel myself close to joining her, my hand wrapping around her neck, applying a little pressure. I know she can manage to hold on as I slam into her one last time.

I roar out as my cum fills her greedy little pussy.

We stay naked, wrapped up in each other, the warmth of the fire and the quiet hum of the radio fading into the background, for a while as we both catch our breath back. I rest my forehead against hers, savouring the intimacy of the moment, her fingers still tangled in my hair.

"Francesca," Unable to stop the smile that tugs at my lips. "This... this feels right."

She nods, a smile spreading across her face, matching mine, her eyes shining with a tenderness that makes my heart ache.

"It does," she whispers. "It really does."

We don't say much after that, and we don't need to. An understanding settles between us as we hold each other, knowing that whatever tomorrow brings, this moment is ours.

The air around us feels different, not with the urgency or passion, but with something peaceful, tranquil—perhaps even fragile.

***

The first light of Christmas morning filters through the windows, casting a glow over the bar. The storm has finally passed, leaving behind a fresh blanket of snow that coats everything in a pristine white. Outside, the world seems as if holding its breath, waiting for whatever is to come next.

I sit up slowly, pulling my shirt back on as I glance over at Francesca. She is still wrapped in the blanket we'd borrowed from the storage room, her hair tousled from sleep, and her eyes half-open—she is undeniably beautiful.

I can't help but think how much has changed in just twenty-four hours.

This time yesterday, I was moping around my childhood home, feeling disconnected from the world and everything in it. And now, here I was, waking up in the bar, with my Pixie beside me.

Last night was unexpected, to say the least. It was something I didn't think I'd ever have again. But now, in the light of day, those doubts and uncertainties have started to creep back in.

"It's Christmas morning," Francesca states, stretching her arms up before wincing slightly as she looks around the bar. With a huge smile on her face she admits, "I've never woken up in a bar on Christmas before."

I chuckle, pulling on my jacket as the early morning chill begins to settle in. "First time for everything, right?"

She rolls her eyes playfully but continues to grin, pulling the blanket tighter around her shoulders.

Her expression is thoughtful, though—her smile doesn't quite reach her eyes. I can see something else there, too. She looks at the windows, at the snow still piled high outside, and lets out a sigh.

"I guess I should head home," she says, her voice a little tentative, as if she isn't entirely sure whether she wants to leave or stay.

Nodding, I feel the same twinge of reluctance but its Christmas; So, her family comes first, right? "Yeah, the roads should be clear enough now. I can drive you in my truck."

I feel a shift in her demeanour. It's subtle at first, just the lift of her eyebrows, a flicker of something in her eyes—confusion, maybe, or disappointment. She looks at me for a long moment before speaking again.

"What did you say?" she asks, her tone calm, but her gaze more focused now.

I blink; taken back by her sudden change in tone. "I said I can drive you home. My truck's parked out back."

There is another beat of silence as she stares at me, and I can see the gears turning in her head. She isn't angry, exactly, but there's some intensity in the way she's looking at me.

"So... you had a truck this whole time?" she asks, her voice quieter now, but the disappointment more evident.

I swallow, not entirely sure where this is going. "Yeah. I mean, it's been parked out back since before the storm hit."

She narrows her eyes slightly as if she is processing something. Then she lets out a sigh. "You could've driven me home last night, then?"

The question catches me off guard. "I... well, I guess I could have," I say, as her words sink in. "But it was snowing pretty hard, and I thought—"

"You didn't think to ask me?" she interrupts, her voice still calm, but there's an edge to it now. "You just assumed I wouldn't want to go home?"

I open my mouth to explain, but I can already see where this was heading. She isn't angry, not in the way she might have been years ago, but she's upset. And that, somehow, feels worse.

"I'm sorry," I say, my voice small now, feeling the gravity of the situation settle in. "I didn't think you'd want to be out in the storm. I just wanted to make sure you were safe."

Francesca shakes her head, her expression letting up a little, but the dismay is still there. "I get that, Heath. I do. But I should've had a choice. You could have at least asked me."

"I know," I admit, rubbing the back of my neck.

We stand there for a moment longer, the silence between us heavy but not hostile. It's more reflective, like we are both trying to figure out what to do next.

I offer her a hand, helping her into her coat, and we make our way toward the door. The freezing morning air rushes in as I open it, the snow outside glistening in the light of dawn.

The drive back to her house is quiet, the silence between us no longer tense but thoughtful.

She sits beside me, her eyes focused on the snow-covered landscape outside the window, her expression unreadable.

I can't tell what she was thinking, but I know she's still processing what happened. The warmth we'd shared last night before feels distant now, like a memory, I want to hold onto but I'm sure how to.

As we pull up to her house, I put the truck in park and look over at her. "Francesca... I really am sorry," hoping she can hear the sincerity in my voice. "I didn't mean to make you feel like you didn't have a choice."

She looks at me for a long moment, her eyes tearing up. "I know you didn't, Heath. But that's what it felt like."

I nod, not knowing what else to say. She opens the door and steps out into the snow, her breath visible in the crisp morning air. I watch her walk toward her front door, her shoulders hunched against the cold. Just before she reaches the door, she stops and turns to look at me.

"I still trust you, Heath," she says quietly, her voice carrying more weight than I expected. "You just need to stop making decisions for me."

"I will," I say again, my voice thick with emotion. "I promise."

She gives me a sharp nod before turning back and heading inside. The door closes behind her, and I sit there for a moment, staring at the house.

The quiet of the morning feels oppressive now. Outside of my truck appears peaceful but inside, I feel anything but.

As I drive away, I can't shake the feeling that I've come close to something—something important, something real—and yet, I almost let it slip through my fingers. I've made mistakes, and I know that. But there is still a chance, I hope, to make things right.

The miles stretch out before me, and with them, the weight of my choices over the years settle heavier in my chest. Last night, I had her in my arms, even if just for a little while. I had a glimpse of what could have been, of what still might be.

If I want to keep her in my life, I have to do better—much better. And I can only hope that she'll give me the chance to prove it.

Chapter 13

Francesca.

Opening the front door of my childhood home, numb from the cold and from everything that just happened. Snow is still stuck to my boots, but I hardly notice it as I step inside, shutting out the chill.

My sisters' laughter drifts from the kitchen, bright and oblivious, and for a moment, I consider sneaking straight upstairs to hide in my room.

"Fran!" Rory's voice rings out, her tone mischievous and full of life, and I know there's no chance of slipping past them unnoticed.

Before I can even take my coat off, my five sisters gather around me, their faces a mix of concern, curiosity, and, in Lottie's case, mild annoyance.

"Late night, was it?" Lottie raises an eyebrow, her perfectly manicured fingers tapping impatiently on her phone screen.

"Yes, late night," I mutter, trying to dodge her gaze as I shrug off my coat. But, of course, I'm not fooling any of them.

"Alright, spill it," says Brimley, cutting right to the point.

I swallow, glancing away, but there's no escaping it. Not here. "Yeah... I... I saw Heath, I accidently bumped into him at a bar, last night."

My voice cracks on that last word, and Brimley reaches out, taking my hand in hers, I know she's doing it, to remind me that no matter what, I'm not alone. The twins, Abby and Annie, exchange a quick, wide-eyed glance, and I can almost hear the unspoken thoughts running between them, ready to pounce on the gossip.

"Wait, you actually saw him?" Annie's eyes are huge, shimmering with curiosity. "Like, in person?"

"And spent the night with him?" Abby adds, winking, though she bites her lip with concern as her eyes search my face. Leave it to the twins to bounce between nosiness and empathy in seconds flat.

I nod, feeling my cheeks flush as the memories of last night—our hands tangled, our whispered words in the dark—flood back to me. But then so does the argument. That jarring, familiar feeling of being on two completely different paths.

"Yep. And then we argued...well, kind of," I say, forcing a shrug. "Some things never change."

They all go quiet, and for a moment, the room is silent except for the ticking of the clock. Then, right on cue, Rory breaks the tension.

"Well, on the bright side, you still got it, Fran," she says, nudging me with her elbow and grinning. "I mean, he's back in town for like, what, a week, let's say? And he's already spending the night."

"Rory!" Brimley scolds, but even she can't hide a small smile. It's impossible not to feel a little lighter around Rory's shameless humour.

"Come on, can't a girl find a silver lining?" Rory grins. "Besides, we haven't even gotten to the juicy part. How was he? Still handsome, tall, and tortured?"

A sad smile plays on my lips as I shake my head, feeling the warmth of my sisters' eyes on me, all of them eager to help, even if they don't know how. "He's still... Heath. Handsome, and, yes, tortured."

"Ugh, he sounds exhausting," Lottie mutters, crossing her arms, and shaking her head. "I don't understand what you see in him, honestly. If he wanted to be with you, he'd be here. What's so complicated about that?"

Her words sting, but she isn't entirely wrong. I know Lottie isn't trying to be harsh—she's just being Lottie, pragmatic and blunt.

She sees the world in black and white, and to her, Heath is simply a foolish, indecisive man. But that isn't how it is for me. It has never been that simple.

"He's... he's not like that," I say softly, not sure I'm believing it myself. "He just... needs something different than I do."

Brimley squeezes my shoulder and leads me over to the sofa. "Let's sit. You can tell us as much—or as little—as you want. No pressure."

I take a deep breath and sink into the cushions, glancing around at their expectant faces. The twins are perched on the arm of the sofa, leaning toward me. Lottie has settled into her usual judgmental-but-curious spot by the door, and Rory is already rifling through her bag for snacks, like she's gearing up for a movie.

"It was... kind of like we'd never been apart," I admit finally. "For a few hours, I just... let myself be in the moment with him. It was stupid, I know, but I just wanted to pretend. Then, this morning, we woke up, and I let my mind overthink, my thoughts race through the past, all of it—everything we didn't agree on, the years of being apart— I let it all, come rushing back."

"Because you think, he wants to run off to every corner of the world and drag you with him?" Lottie huffs, rolling her eyes.

"Yes, something like that," I murmur, tracing a pattern on the arm of the sofa. "He's still Heath. I mean we didn't talk about it, but I know him, he wants a life that's big and loud and full of adventure. He wants me wherever he needs me and I…" My voice cracks, but I forced myself to continue, "… I just want him. Here."

Brimley's face softens, and she takes my hand. "Franny, there's nothing wrong with that. Wanting to do you, doesn't make you less than him or anyone else."

"She's right," Abby pipes in. "And for what it's worth, he's kind of a jerk for expecting you to just… fit into his life without making room for yours, the first time round."

"Exactly!" Annie adds, nodding enthusiastically. "It's like he wanted a sidekick, not a partner."

I feel a laugh bubble up, weak but genuine. "Only you two would put it like that."

The twins grin. I'm still heartbroken, but for now, I feel like maybe, just maybe, I don't have to carry it alone.

"Well," Rory says, her face full of mischief as she leans toward me, "Since you're back and Heath is… wherever he is, I think we should do our presents to cheer you up. It is Christmas day, after all."

"Presents." I try to sound excited for them.

"Yep! And guess what?" Rory holds up a small, crinkled bag with slips of paper inside. "You're going to pick first."

It's our family Christmas tradition that every year, we place our names into a bag and whoever you pick out of the bag is the person who gets the first present of Christmas.

"Alright, alright." I give in, reaching into the bag. It's a small distraction, but it feels nice to be part of something light-hearted, something that had nothing to do with Heath or heartbreak.

I unfold the piece of paper and read the name with a faint smile. "Rory."

"Perfect!" Rory claps her hands together, looking pleased. "But I warn you—I'm expecting big things."

After Rory opens her present, the rest of my sisters and my parents dive into unwrapping their gifts. Their voices overlap as they bicker over what would be considered 'fair' to give.

Brimley is talking about handmade gifts, while the twins are on about plotting something ridiculous for next year involving reindeer antlers and glitter. Even Lottie looks amused, though she is pretending not to care.

Watching them, I feel a pang of gratitude, mixed with sadness. Heath would never understand this—this cozy, chaotic sense of home, of belonging. To him, life is out there, in the wide-open spaces, in the foreign streets and train stations. For me, it's here, in these messy, ridiculous moments with my sisters.

Brimley must have seen the faraway look in my eyes because she wraps her arm around my shoulders. "Whatever happens with Heath," she says quietly, "we're here, Fran. You've always got us."

"Yeah," I whisper, my voice thick with emotion. "I know."

And I do know it, deep down. I'm not alone, not really. Even if my heart aches, even if I feel torn between my past with Heath and my present here, I know I have a family that would catch me if I fell. A family that makes me laugh, even when I think I can't.

Chapter 14

Francesca

Sitting cross-legged on my bed, the late afternoon winter sun streams through the window, casting a warm glow on the room I've known my entire life. The faded wallpaper, the clutter of old memories, and the worn-out furniture feels like a suffocating cocoon. It's a place that once brought comfort but now feels like a reminder of how stuck I am. Everything around me seems unchanged, yet everything inside me is unravelling.

The more I think about Christmas Eve with Heath, the more I realize how much I overreacted. I wipe a tear that slips down my cheek. When I really put it all into perspective, we were both in shock that night. Neither of us had been thinking clearly. And maybe... *maybe I'd flown off the handle.*

Even though I overreacted, it doesn't change the bigger problem. It isn't just about the misunderstanding in the bar. Heath wanted to travel the world, to explore, to be free, and I... *I couldn't.* I had my life here, my responsibilities, my job. We weren't just dealing with one night of confusion.

Our whole lives were clashing.

A knock on the door startles me, and I quickly wipe my face, though I know the redness in my eyes will betray me. Annie peeks her head in, her eyes immediately narrowing as she sees me sitting there, looking a mess.

"Franny, what's going on?" she asks gently, stepping into the room. "You've been moping around the house for two days. I know something's up."

I try to laugh, but it comes out as a shaky breath. "I'm fine. Just... thinking too much, I guess. Pacing down memory lane and all that."

Annie crosses her arms, raising an eyebrow in disbelief. "You're pacing around because you're upset about something, and I'm pretty sure I know what—or who—it is." She sits down beside me on the bed, her voice softening. "It's Heath, isn't it?"

At the sound of his name, my chest tightens, and I can't stop the flood of emotions that have been building up. My throat burns as I try to speak, but the words get stuck. Instead, all that comes out is a broken, "I don't know what to do."

Annie's face softens, and without a word, she reaches out and pulls me into a hug. That simple gesture is all it takes for the dam to break. I sob into her shoulder, the weight of everything I've been holding inside crashing down on me all at once. I can't hold it in anymore.

"I love him," I choke out between sobs. "I love him so much, but I ruined it, Annie. I completely ruined everything."

Annie rubs my back, not saying anything at first, just letting me cry. After a moment, she pulls back slightly to look at me, her face full of concern. "Franny, what happened?"

I wipe my eyes with the back of my hand, struggling to compose myself enough to explain. "I freaked out, Annie. That night at the bar, when I realized he could've driven me home, I just lost it. I thought he was trying to trap me there, to keep me. But the more I think about it, the more I realize he wasn't doing anything wrong. I was just... scared."

"Scared of what?" Annie asks, her voice calm and steady.

"Scared that he's going to leave again. Scared that I'll never be enough for him," I admit, my voice breaking. "He wants to travel, to see the world. And I can't. I've spent my whole life building something here. I can't just walk away from all of this. And even if I could... I don't know how to make it work. We're too different."

Annie frowns, tilting her head. "Do you really think you and Heath are too different, Franny? Or is it that you're scared of what it means to let go of your control? Because that's what it sounds like to me."

I stare at the floor, my vision blurry from tears. "I don't know. Maybe. I just know that I pushed him away. I didn't trust him, and now I'm terrified it's too late. I love him so much, but what if I can't give him the life he wants? What if I'm just holding him back?"

Huffing loudly as she takes my hand. "Franny, you're not holding him back. You're holding *yourself* back. You're so focused on what you can't do that you're not seeing all the possibilities. Why can't you both make it work? Why does it have to be one or the other?"

"Because I have responsibilities here," I say, my voice rising in frustration. "We built this company together. I can't just up and leave. I have to be here, with all of you."

She sighs again, her voice gentle but firm. "Franny, we built the company together, yes. But it's not a prison. You're allowed to want more than just stability. You're allowed to want both. You can work remotely—you've set up everything to make that possible. You could be with Heath and still manage the company from anywhere in the world."

I shake my head, the tears still falling. "But what if it's too much? What if I fail? What if I let everyone down?"

Annie squeezes my hand tighter. "You won't fail. And even if things don't go perfectly, we're here. You're not in this alone. Brimley can handle the day-to-day stuff, Abby's got the organization covered, and Rory, well... Rory's Rory, comic relief, but we'll all be fine, and so will you."

I look at her, my voice barely above a whisper. "You really think I can do this?"

Brushing a tear off my cheek with the swipe of her thumb, "Yes, I really do. You've been the strong one for so long, always doing everything by the book. But maybe now it's time for you to take a chance, to let go a little. You love Heath, and he clearly loves you too. This is your chance to have both—a life with him and your career. You don't have to choose one or the other. You're allowed to have both."

Her words wash over me, and for the first time, I feel a flicker of hope. Could I really make this work? Could I find a way to be with Heath without giving up everything I've built? The thought is terrifying, but also... exhilarating.

"I don't know what I'd do without you," I say, my voice cracking as another tear slides down my face.

Annie smiles, her eyes warm. "You don't have to figure this out alone, Franny. We're all here for you. But you have to give yourself permission to go after what you want. Life's too short to let fear hold you back."

I nod, sniffling as I try to steady my breath. She's right. I've been so focused on the fear of losing control, on the fear of not being enough for Heath, that I haven't stopped to think about what I am truly capable of. I can do this. I can have both.

Taking a deep breath, I wipe the last of my tears away and sit up straighter. "Okay," I say, my voice stronger now. "I'm going to do it. I'm going to go after Heath, and I'm going to make this work. I love him, and I'm not letting fear stop me anymore."

Annie's face lights up with a proud smile. "That's my girl. Go get him, Fran."

I laugh through the remnants of my tears, feeling lighter than I have in days. "I will. Thank you, Annie. I mean it."

She stands, pulling me into one last hug. "Anytime. Now go, and make sure to tell him how you really feel. And don't forget—this time, you're allowed to want more than just 'safe.' You're allowed to want it all."

As I watch her leave, I feel a new sense of determination settle over me. This isn't about just making things right with Heath. This is about taking control of my life—choosing what I want, not just what feels safe.

I stand up from the bed, a surge of energy running through me. I have to fix things with Heath, and I have to show him that I'm ready to build a future with him. It isn't too late.

And I am not going to lose him without a fight.

Chapter 15

Heath

The days after Christmas at any bar are a rare scene. The places are always dimly lit, the building is usually nearly empty, except for a few locals nursing their beers like the world outside isn't covered in fairy lights and snow.

So, I've spent the last few days hiding out here, at the bar, after my last conversation with Francesca, which had ended…well, not how I'd hoped. I hadn't planned to see her. I'd come back to town just to spend the holidays with my folks and Marlee, but fate gave her back to me. And then immediately took her away… Just like always.

I sip my beer, glancing out at the snow falling again beyond the bar window. Francesca has always been right, in her own way—she knew what she wanted, where she wanted to be. But, as for me, I've never been able to shake the itch for something bigger, something that pulled me beyond the place I've grown up in. And because of that, our lives have never really fit together.

Still, I can't stop thinking about her. Seeing her again has brought everything back—the good and the complicated.

The way she looked at me with those big, soulful eyes, like she could see right through all my extensive ideas to the parts I try to keep hidden... I know it wasn't fair to ask her to change her whole life five years ago, just as much as it wasn't fair for her to ask me to stay.

The bar door creaks open, and I turn, expecting to see Frank, another bartender, but instead, I nearly spit out my beer. Francesca stands there, snowflakes in her dark hair, cheeks flushed from the cold, her leather jacket hanging off one shoulder like she rushed here without thinking twice. My heart skips, and I set my beer down, bracing myself for whatever is about to happen.

"Heath." Her voice is breathless, a little wild. She takes a few steps toward me, and I swear every pair of eyes in the bar is suddenly locked on us.

"Franny." I lean back in my seat, giving her a small, cautious smile. "What are you doing here?"

She swallows, looking down for a second before meeting my gaze. "I came to talk to you. Actually, no. I came to beg."

The corner of my mouth twitches. I can't help it. Francesca, the most stubborn woman I've ever met, begging? That is something I haven't seen before.

"Begging, huh?" I try to keep my tone light, playful, but the look in her eyes stops me cold. She's serious. I can see it in the way her hands twist together, how her eyes are already a little red, like she's been trying not to cry.

"Don't laugh," she mutters, frowning. "I mean it."

I motion to the seat across from me. "Alright then, Pixie. I'm all ears."

She looks hesitant, but eventually slides into the seat, setting her jacket down beside her. She stares at her hands, and for a moment, I think she might get up and bolt. But then, she takes a deep breath and looks up at me.

"Heath," she begins, then pauses, wringing her hands again. "I know we don't... I know we've never seen eye-to-eye on some things. I get that you want a life that's... bigger, more exciting. I know I've always been the one who wants stability, who wants to stay. But..."

She takes a deep breath, and I lean in, giving her my full attention. It feels like we've had this conversation a hundred times, but I can't help the way my heart picks up just watching her.

"But I don't want to spend the rest of my life wondering," she says, her voice barely above a whisper. "Wondering what it would have been like if I'd tried. If we'd tried."

I can feel my heart thudding in my chest, but I keep my face neutral. "What are you saying, Franny?"

She takes another breath, then lets the words tumble out, fast and unguarded. "I'm saying... I'm saying I'm tired of fighting. I want a second chance. I don't care if you want to see the world. I want to see it with you. I'll go. I don't know, I'll pack a bag and figure it out. I'll try, Heath, because I'd rather be out of my comfort zone with you than drowning without you."

She looks down, like she's embarrassed, and I can't help but smile. I know she's spent years building the life she wanted—one that doesn't include a constant stream of boarding passes and new cities. The idea that she'd give that up for me, even for a little while, is overwhelming.

But still. I can't just say yes that easily. That isn't us.

"Wait, let me get this straight." I lean forward, crossing my arms on the table. "You're telling me that you, Francesca-with-a-five-year-plan, want to drop everything, go globetrotting with me, and, I don't know, live out of a backpack?"

Her cheeks flush, but she nods, defiant. "Yes. I'll live out of a backpack, or a suitcase, whatever. I'll stay in those terrible hostels you like; I'll even eat... street food." She says it like it's some kind of penance, and I have to bite back a laugh.

"Oh, you'll eat street food?" I say, my tone full of mock surprise. "Next, you're going to tell me you're ready to give up those spreadsheets you love so much."

She narrows her eyes, clearly fighting the urge to laugh, and leans in, lowering her voice like she's confessing a great secret. "Yes, even the spreadsheets."

That does it. I burst out laughing, and after a moment, so does she. She looks down, biting her lip to stifle her laughter, and when she looks back up, she has that look—the one that always got to me, the one that is a mix of vulnerability and bravery, like she's showing me her heart and daring me to break it.

"Look, Heath," she says softly, her laughter fading. "I don't know if I'm good at this. I don't know if I can be the kind of person who's okay with uncertainty. But I'm willing to try. For you. If it means I don't have to say goodbye to you again."

I stare at her, my mind racing. Part of me wants to say 'yes' right there, to sweep her up in my arms and tell her we'll go anywhere she wants. But another part of me, the cautious part, the part that knows Francesca better than anyone, holds back.

"Franny," I say quietly, reaching across the table to take her hand. "Are you sure about this? Because this is... your life, you know? Your routines, your plans. Your sisters. I don't want you to wake up in some random country a year from now and realize this isn't what you want."

She squeezes my hand, her face serious, and nods. "I know. But... I also know that the life I've been building without you feels empty. All those things—my plans, my routines—they don't mean anything if you're not in them."

I looked down at our hands, her small fingers wrapped around mine, and feel the weight of everything we've been through—the breakups, the arguments, the nights we've spent missing each other. And here she is, in this small, dark bar on Christmas, offering me everything.

"So, you'd really do it?" I ask, still smiling. "You'd live out of a suitcase, eat sketchy street food, and give up your sacred five-year plan?"

She laughs, rolling her eyes. "Yes, Heath. Even the sacred five-year plan."

A warmth spreads through me that I hadn't felt in years. I've loved Francesca since the moment I met her, even when I didn't want to admit it to myself, and here she was, willing to give up everything to be with me.

"Well," I say, squeezing her hand and giving her a lopsided smile. "If you're willing to eat questionable food and live in hostels, then I'd better get used to grocery lists and, you know, maybe planning a little. For you."

She looks at me, her eyes shining, and I know we're both imagining it—this wild life we can build together, a mix of chaos and comfort, of wandering and home. It won't be perfect, and we'll probably drive each other insane more often than not. But maybe, just maybe, that's okay.

"So," she whispers, leaning closer. "Is that a yes?"

I grin, pulling her hand to my lips, and brushing a kiss across her knuckles. "It's a yes, Franny. And for the record, I'd go anywhere if it meant I didn't have to say goodbye to you again."

Her face breaks into a smile, and before I know it, she's in my arms, her laughter filling the empty bar. I hold her close, breathing her in, and for the first time in years, I feel like I am exactly where I'm meant to be.

The bartender clears his throat. I've been so caught up with my Pixie, I hadn't heard him come in. We break apart, both of us laughing like teenagers caught sneaking a kiss.

She's mine, and I 'am hers, and that is all I need.

"Alright, let's get packing, baby."

Epilogue

Heath

I set my phone on a makeshift stand—a half-empty coffee cup—and wait as the familiar ring tone fills the small kitchen.

Sunlight filters through the window, casting warm streaks across the countertop as I adjust the angle, making sure Marlee can see the view outside. The Australian coast stretches out just beyond the sliding glass door, waves crashing against sunlit rocks, blue sky stretching endlessly above.

"About time, Mr. Jetsetter!" Marlee's face pops up on the screen, grinning as she settles into view. She looks more or less the same as when I last seen her months ago, though her hair is a bit shorter, and she's wearing one of those oversized sweaters she always wears when it gets too cold back home.

"Hey, sis." I lean back, crossing my arms with a smirk. "Miss me?"

"Not as much as I miss annoying you," she shoots back, raising an eyebrow. "So, what's it like in paradise? Just out there sipping cocktails and surfing all day?"

"Not exactly." I laugh, glancing back at the stunning view. "Though I did attempt to surf last week. Got wiped out in about two seconds flat."

She laughs, shaking her head. "Should have figured. So where are you now? You and Francesca are still in...?"

"Still in Australia, yeah. We're in a tiny town called Byron Bay right now. Kind of a hippie, beachy vibe. Perfect for just slowing down, getting work done, you know?" I shrug, trying to sound casual, but the truth is, every day here feels a bit like a dream.

Marlee looks skeptical, her eyebrow lifting. "Since when do you 'slow down'? Last I heard, you were working on a new app. Don't tell me you've learned to relax?"

I roll my eyes, unable to hide my grin. "Hey, I can relax. But yes, I'm working on something new. Just a small project, keeping it low-key." I lean forward, lowering my voice like I am letting her in on a secret. "It's an app to help travellers find workspaces, cafés with Wi-Fi, stuff like that."

She laughs. "You're literally making an app to help people *not* relax. Sounds about right."

"Look, I just... I saw the need, okay? It's useful. I mean, half the time Francesca's working on a project, we're hopping between random cafés, trying to find a spot with decent internet."

Marlee's eyes soften, her smile widening. "I can't believe she actually left her home office fortress to travel with you."

I laugh, nodding. "Honestly, neither can I. I still half-expect her to wake up one morning and realize she left behind her color-coded calendar and run back to the States. But she's adapted... she's even stopped organizing her emails by colour."

"Whoa." Marlee feigns shock, putting a hand to her heart. "That's huge. She must really love you."

"Or I've just worn her down," I say, grinning. "But yes, I think she's enjoying it. She's still on top of things with her sisters' and company—sometimes we'll be on the road, and she's FaceTiming them or working on her laptop while we're parked at some lookout point. She's even got Brimley in charge of weekly 'remote team check-ins.' It's terrifying how much they get done without ever setting foot in an office."

"Spoken like a man who has no idea how to properly schedule his life," Marlee teases, giving me a mockingly sympathetic look.

"Hey, I'm organized," I shoot back, though even I can hear how unconvincing it sounds. "I mean, I'm here working, aren't I? Got this app coming along, we've got places to see... What more do you want?"

"Uh-huh. And you're totally not just living off Francesca's organization skills?"

I grin, leaning back. "Maybe a little. But it works. And she's, you know, happy."

"She looks happy. You both do. It's good to see."

"Yeah, she really is," I say, looking out the window. "And, honestly, I didn't know if this would work. Thought maybe she'd get bored of it, that it wouldn't be... enough for her. But here we are, four months in, and she's still here."

"You sound surprised," Marlee says, smiling knowingly.

I shrug, running a hand through my hair. "I am, a bit. I mean, Francesca was always... steady, you know? She was the one with the five-year plan, she had her life mapped out, while I was always the one pulling in some wild direction. But now... she's different. She's *us,* I guess—both grounded and open to whatever happens next."

Marlee nods thoughtfully. "Sounds like she's got a pretty major influence in her life. And hey, she might have loosened up a bit, but don't let that fool you—she's probably still tracking every expense and taking notes on every location for her sisters."

"Oh, absolutely. Just last week, she was taking photos of a coworking space here, claiming she was 'scouting international office styles' for the company. It's hilarious."

Marlee laughs, her eyes shining. "So basically, she's the same Francesca—just with a passport and a much better tan."

"Pretty much," I agree, chuckling. "But she's also... freer, I think. She's started talking about the places she wants to see, like Japan, and Italy. It's like she finally let herself imagine a life without limits. And I think that's what makes it work."

"Well, I've always loved her," Marlee says, her voice soft. "You two are perfect together, even if it took you both a while to see it."

I grin, feeling that familiar tug of happiness when I think about Francesca. "Yeah, she's kind of incredible. And believe me, I know how lucky I am that she took this chance on me."

Marlee raises an eyebrow, "Oh, please. You act like she's the only one who's changed. You're the one who left behind a solo, no-strings life for a relationship and an app that helps people. You're practically a different person."

I scoff, shrugging off her words with a laugh. "Hey, don't get ahead of yourself. I'm still me. I'm just... less terrible with logistics now."

"Sure, sure," Marlee says, her smile widening. "But honestly, Heath, I'm really proud of you. Watching you take this leap, settle down without *settling*, it's... inspiring."

I feel a familiar warmth at her words, grateful for her support. "Thanks, Mar. I don't think I could've done this without you pushing me to be less of an idiot about things, you know?"

"That's what sisters are for," she says, smiling. "And I always knew you'd find your place. It just so happens your place is, you know, everywhere."

"Sounds about right," I say, looking out at the waves again, feeling that thrill of freedom mixed with stability—something I never thought I'd find. "I guess I'm just lucky that Francesca was willing to go everywhere with me."

It was true—Francesca and I had both given up something, both let go of pieces of our old lives to make room for each other. And somehow, we built something better than I could ever imagine.

"So, what's next?" Marlee asks, looking curious. "Are you two just going to keep traveling, or is there, you know, a plan?"

I laugh, leaning back. "A plan? Mar, you know me better than that. There's no plan. Not really. We're just… seeing what happens next. For now, it's Australia. Then… maybe Japan. Maybe Italy. Francesca keeps talking about Venice."

"Oh, that's perfect for you," she says, rolling her eyes. "The man who has never met a plan he didn't immediately throw out, and the woman who probably has backup files of her backup files."

"Exactly," I reply, grinning. "That's why it works."

Marlee smiles again, and I can see the warmth in her eyes. "You're happy, Heath. And that's all I've ever wanted for you."

"I am," I say, feeling the truth of it deep in my chest. "And don't worry, we'll come visit soon. Francesca is dying to see you again."

Marlee laughs. "Good. Can't wait to see you both. And Heath? … Get a haircut!"

The End.

Author Note.

Hey lovelies,
Thank you for taking the time to read Dashing Through The Snow.
I really hope you liked Franny and Heath's story!
My lost souls looking for one another to make them whole again, they just needed a second chance and time to fix their mess.
I adore being in this world, Franny and her sisters make my heart sing in delight. The way they bounce of each other, pretend to be annoyed but love each other fiercely... It's sister goals for sure.
Keep swiping to read the first few chapters of Brimley's Story (Also out by Laura Rush section of this Ebook)
Moving on ...
It's been a jam-packed year for me, and next year is looking similar.
(Insert holiday to the New York for one please)
I'd love it, if you ~~stalked~~ stuck around soooo ...
If you want to keep up to date on what's coming next follow me on socials:
@authorlaurarush
Until the next time,
Yours always,
Laura XoXo
If you enjoyed my book, I would love and appreciate it if you could leave me an honest review on Amazon or Goodreads.

Also, out by Laura Rush

Ready to meet Brimley Harris?

What do you get when Cindy Lou Who meets a grumpy Grinchy wine maker?

So, This is Christmas is what!

It's the Rom-Com, road trip to from Paris to New York. Read the first few chapters here –

Chapter 1 - Shaun

Name me something worse than a cancelled flight due to a small dusting of snow on the runway.

Oh, you can't? No worries, I'll tell you.

Fucking Christmas, that's what!

I should be happy— no, *delighted*—my flight's been cancelled on my way home to New York City. I cannot stand Christmas; the whole thing freaking sucks. Waste of time and money if you ask me. So-called families gather for the 'most wonderful time of year,' the giving of gifts, the decorations, the crazed shoppers, the over-the-top consumption of food... the list is endless.

But even my *bah humbug* ass cannot miss this year. I needed to get home, like, yesterday. My dearest brother decided to drop down on one knee and propose to his darling Kimmy a week ago, and my family thought it would be a grand idea to throw a Christmas Eve celebration party at their house.

I stretch out my legs in front of me, brushing a hand through my hair. My head's pounding with stress; I try cracking my neck from side to side in an attempt to release some tension in it. Turning towards the windows to my left, I watch the snow pick up momentum and fall to the ground.

Looks like I won't be home tonight either. *Fuck!*

Pulling out my iPhone from my pocket, I search for Dad's name and hit the call button. *Here we go… Welcome to hell.*

"Have you arrived yet?" My dad's voice booms down my receiver.

I sigh loudly. "I'm great, Dad, thanks for asking. And no, is the answer to your question. My flight from Paris was cancelled due to snow and it looks like my next flight will be as well." My response is clipped, my annoyance clear.

"Shaun, it's once a year I ask you to be home. You've had three-hundred-and-sixty-five days to plan this. More so, you know how important this year's gathering will be," he snaps back.

Didn't he just hear me? I cannot help, nor predict, the weather forecast!

"I am fully aware of that, Dad, but it's out of my hands!" I say through gritted teeth. My father and I have never seen eye to eye; Mom reckons it's because we're so alike. How she puts up with his moody ass, I will never know.

"I do not care how you do it, Shaun. Christmas Eve is a few days away, so by hook or crook, you get yourself here and with the best god damn smile on your face when you arrive. I won't have you spoiling it for Jack and Kimberly!" he shouts back at me and hangs up.

I stare at my phone in my hand for a moment, my mouth slack in shock. wondering why the hell he wants me there anyway— the man clearly cannot stand me. Stuffing it back into my pocket and picking up my rucksack off the floor, I walk to find the nearest bar. I need a strong drink to drown my sorry self in.

As I turn to my right, I bump into the mother of all Christmas angels. A petite, chestnut-haired woman looks up at me. She shyly smiles while pushing her glasses back up the bridge of her nose and her bright, ocean- blue eyes bore into mine. I notice how they accentuate the freckles that dot across her nose and rosy cheeks. I step back and my eyes squint now looking at her in full form. I would like to take back my previous comment of 'a Christmas angel' and replace it with a Christmas malfunction. *What the fuck is she wearing?*

A white, light- up 'I heart Xmas' sweater blinds me with twinkling, flashing lights. She's paired it with green leggings and black boots. It takes me a moment to realise that she's speaking to me; I watch her lips move for another second before shaking my head.

"I am sorry, what did you say? Your sweater hindered my eyes so much it temporarily shut down my ability to hear and think," I say, my lips curling in disgust.

She smirks back up at me. "I see. Well, I was saying I'm sorry for bumping into you. But now I am not so sorry. Merry almost-Christmas Eve to you, good Sir." She singsongs the last part out and walks away.

Merry almost-Christmas Eve?

God, if you can hear me, just zap a lightning bolt straight through my head, please.

***

"Good evening, passengers. This is the pre-boarding announcement for flight 89B to New York City. We are now inviting those passengers with small children, and any passengers requiring special assistance, to begin boarding at this time. Please have your boarding pass and

identification ready. Regular boarding will begin in approximately ten minutes' time. Thank you."

Downing the last of my scotch, I stand, a little too wobbly for my liking. Instantly worrying about the fact, I might be too drunk to get on the plane, I signal the bartender to grab me a bottle of water, paying on my card, before heading towards the terminal.

Patience has never been my thing. Even less so when I have had a drink. I push past some happy families hugging loved one's goodbye for the holidays, and march towards where I need to be, cursing and flipping the bird to unhappy people who get in my way. Feeling relieved this hell I have been thrown into is nearing its end, I stand in the queue to get onto the plane. Pulling out my phone, I text Jack— my younger brother, and the favourite child— to tell him that I'm about to catch my flight to New York. I hear a voice pipe up behind me and I let out an audible groan.

"Oh, look who it is; it's Mr Grinch himself!" I can practically hear the smile stretching across her jolly face.

***

Chapter 2 - Brimley

I cover my smile with the book I have in my hand as Grinchy whirls around in my direction. Listen, I am all about bringing the Christmas spirit to all who need it, and Mr Grinch needs it desperately.

It is the season for giving, after all.

He doesn't look like the green haired Grinch I know and love—in-fact, he looks the complete opposite, like he literally walked out of a Vogue magazine shoot. His broad shoulders flex underneath his tight t-shirt as he clenches and unclenches his fists. That beautiful face should be off- putting considering the scowl it wears right now, but it's not. Thick eyebrows that are drawn together nearly cover his long, dark eyelashes and deep brown eyes. He has a perfect shaped nose and kissable lips, with the final addition of a strong shaped jaw line. *He's like fucking Hercules.*

I snap out of my perving, removing my bottom lip from my teeth and ask him, "What were you saying? Sorry."

"I see you're still wearing that offensive sweater," he says in a dry voice, while putting on a pair of sunglasses.

"What's with the glasses?" I ask, immediately regretting it, knowing his next response will be something to insult my lovely, hand-knitted jumper.

Raising a brow at me, he sighs heavily. "Isn't it obvious, Fruit Loop?" He stretches out his free hand to flick a light on my jumper. *True Grinch style.*

I bite my bottom lip again to cover my incoming smile.

"That's the second time you've complimented my sweater. You want one, too?" I say while not looking at him and pulling my bag in front of me to pretend I'm looking for something. I'm not, but he's so fun to mess with. "I'm sure I have a matching one in my bag; you can totally have it if you want!"

"*Urh, God, it's me again. Listen, about that lightning bolt I asked you for earlier; if you could just do it already, that would be grand,*" he mutters under his breath. I glance up to see him staring up at the ceiling, eyes closed and hands in the prayer position in front of his chest. I hide another laugh with my hand.

A lady's voice interrupts my next comeback. "Excuse me, sir, ma'am— can I see your boarding passes?" I look over Grinchy's shoulder to see a slender air hostess looking at us both.

"Oh, thank God! That's a better idea," he grumbles, and turns to hand his ticket to the lady.

"And your wife's ticket, sir?" she points at me. I laugh aloud and grab Grinchy's arm before he can respond to her.

"Excuse my husband. He's very tired and we are both eager to get home to our children, Joseph, and Joy," I say, smiling sweetly at her. I hand my boarding pass over while Mr Grinch gapes at me, opened-mouthed. She wishes us both a Merry Christmas and hopes we will be reunited with our children soon. I pull at his arm, ignoring the tingles I feel from touching him, and drag him towards the plane.

Snapping out of his trance, he halts us both on the spot before shouting, "You're a fucking crazy woman!" I laugh in response.

In my best baby-talk voice, I say, "Nooow, where's that Christmaaas spirit gooone? Heeey hubby, you don't want our children to see you all grumpy this year, do you?"

"Just stay away from me, Fruit Loop, okay?" His brows furrow as he frostily points his finger at my nose. I pretend to bite it and his eyes widen before he turns on his heel and stomps down the tunnel.

My smile stretches across my face, and I turn to follow him onto the plane.

I read Seat 68B on my ticket before handing it over to an air hostess and stuffing my book into my bag. She says something while I glance around to try and find my seat. Too embarrassed about not paying attention to her to ask her what she said, I head towards the economy section. Hopefully, my seat neighbour will let me have the window seat instead. With it being a nine-hour flight, I need to be able to look out the window, even if it is pitch black outside.

Finally finding my seat, I turn towards the grumpy face looking up at me from his seat next to the window and break out into a smile while my insides melt.

Placing a hand to my chest, I stare into his hateful eyes and wink. "Jingle my bells, this is a Christmas miracle!"

***

Chapter 3 - Shaun

I am being punished. God is breaking me for making too many requests.

That is, it, I am getting off this plane! There is no way in hell that I am spending the next nine hours sat next to fucking Cindy Lou Who herself. I stand up abruptly, snatching my bag off the ground.

"Get out of my way, Fruit Loop. I am getting off," I snap at her. Staring into her eyes, I hope my anger radiates through her body and the lights on her sweater catch flames, burning it to the ground in front of me. *Now, that would be a Christmas miracle.*

The air hostess comes into view from behind Fruit Loop and asks if there is a problem. She tells me I need to sit down and buckle up because we' re ready for take-off. Fruit Loop doesn't take her eyes off me the entire time.

"Yeah, there's a problem— either find me another seat or I'm getting off this fucking plane!" I erupt at her. I know I'm being a dick but that has been my go-to armour my whole life, so why stop now, right?

The air hostess gasps loudly at my tone before fixing her face into a stern look. "Sir, I will not tolerate you speaking to me like that. There are no other seats and unfortunately, we are about to take off. So, I'm going to ask you again, please take your seat and put your belt on before I call in security."

The captain's announcement comes over the speakers of the plane, informing us all we are about to take off, and I huff my annoyance to them both before sitting down in my seat again and stuffing my bag under my chair.

Fruit Loop must notice my empty level of Christmas spirit and chooses not to look or speak to me again for the next hour.

***

Chapter 4 - Brimley

*'So, this is Christmas
And what have you done?
Another year over
And a new one just begun*

*And so this is Christmas
I hope you have fun
The near and the dear one
The old and the young.'*

I am mid-way listening to the all-time greatest ever Christmas song when my headphones are viciously ripped from my ears.

"Please, I'm begging you to stop. *Please.*"

I scowl over at Grinchy who's holding one end of my earphones in his hand.

"Give me that back, you scrooge." I lean across him to get the other earphone out of his vice grip.

"No. You've been singing the same song on repeat for the last thirty minutes and I can't take much more of it." His eyes plead with me to stop, and I grin back at him. "So, what can I sing then?"

He tilts his head to the side and dryly replies, "Nothing."

Raising my brow and throwing him a questioning gaze. "Well, what do you propose we do instead?"

Shuffling his butt further away towards the window, he side-eyes me in horror, shaking his head. "We? There is no *we,* Fruit Loop." He pauses when his arm hits the window and he glances towards it, sighing loudly because he can't put more distance between us. He continues, "You can't sing, and I need sleep, so if you could be a doll and be quiet for a while, THAT would suit me perfectly."

I throw my head back laughing, then roll my eyes dramatically at him. "That's booooring," I drag out.

"Do not care," he grumbles under his breath, then closes his eyes.

Leaning towards him, I whisper, "Psst." He ignores me, of course, so I psst" again, this time poking him in his shoulder. Again, he ignores me.

Throwing my hands up in the air, I sigh in defeat. "Okay, fine, you win. But just for the record," I pause when he opens one eye at me, "I *can* sing. Not perfectly, but I can."

Huffing at me, he turns in my direction to face me. "My ears are still bleeding, and my eyes... can't you turn off those flashing lights on your sweater?" He points a finger at the green twinkling light on my breast.

I giggle. "No, I cannot," I say whilst crossing my arms over my chest.

Grumbling some more incoherent words at me, I hear him say something along the lines of *'Stupid Christmas, stupid sweater.'*

"Well, Fruit Loop, apparently you and that hideous jumper will not let me sleep. You can't keep your mouth shut, so what do you propose we do instead?" A hint of teasing comes from his last words, and I feel the need to squeeze my legs shut. I lick my lips as I stare at his plump ones.

"Urh, well–" I'm about to answer his question when a head pops up between the gap of our seats. A woman with blonde hair, styled in a pixie cut, grins at me widely before turning her head towards Mr Grinch.

"Don't mind me, but you could exchange names." She beams at us, her tone excited, like she's enjoying the mounting tension between him and me.

I nod slowly at her before turning to him, holding out my hand for him to shake. "Brimley Sadie Harris, but everyone calls me Brim."

He grumbles, *this is nonsense,* before reluctantly taking my hand in his and announcing his name. "Shaun Dawson." His eyes hold mine while the rest of his face is expressionless. My mind begins to wonder why he hasn't let go of my hand yet, although it doesn't feel uncomfortable, It's oddly comforting.

The pixie cut girl speaks up again, breaking our trance." The exchanging of names has just begun; soon the mating dance will commence. Though lucky enough to travel to many places in my life and have seen many wonders, this could just well be the greatest one of all."

Her voice is full of excitement, as she holds up her Dictaphone close to her mouth.

Shaun leans forward and taps her shoulder, causing her to stop and press the pause button on the side. "What are you doing?" His words come out clipped while his nostrils flare.

"I'm making a documentary." She shrugs her shoulders and looks at us like we should have known that's what she's doing.

His hand grips mine tighter as he shouts, "Oh, for fuck's sake!" It causes all the passengers to turn and look at us. Unsure what to do in this exact moment, I just rub my thumb softly over the top of his hand. You know, to comfort him in his hour of need, not because I am desperate to hold his hand longer or anything like that. *It's what the Baby Jesus would have wanted, right?*

Shaun's lips pinch together as a pained look crosses his face. Scratching the back of his neck, he mumbles, "This is just perfect; I'm stuck on a goddamn plane for the next eight hours with a David Attenborough wanna-be and Mrs Claus."

Squeezing his hand, his head whips over in my direction, like he's just put two and two together and realised we are still holding hands.

"It's okay. Shaun. My lights can turn off and I'm sure–" I nod my head to our narrator's direction in front of us and mouth silently, "–will get bored soon." I reluctantly let go of his hand to flip the bottom of my jumper over and press the button, turning the lights off.

Softening his features, he gives me his first real smile. "Thanks. Uh, I'm sorry. It's been a difficult day, that's all."

***

Chapter 5 - Shaun

It always takes so long to calm down my nerves when I'm irate. I feel them swirling around inside my stomach, and I can't seem to get my hands to stop trembling. Dragging my sweaty palms up and down my trousers, I take a few deep breaths. *In and out. In and out.*

It's not working though, so I lean over and grab Brim's free hand. A small gasp leaves her, but she quickly gets back to rubbing her thumb over the top of my hand like before, without uttering a word to me. I know it's strange, right? To hold a stranger's hand on a plane, especially since you haven't been that welcoming and kind to them. But her calm, quiet presence right now is the only thing stopping me from running to the back of the plane and opening the door, before jumping to certain death.

I hate this time of year. The thought of facing my father and living under the same roof as him again, even for just a few days, pushes me to breaking point. I just don't understand why he can't treat me like Jack.

"What do you do for work?" Brim's soft voice pulls me out of my thoughts, and she turns to face me straight on, lifting her legs up to sit cross legged. Giving me a small smile while gently rubbing my hands with hers as if they are cold, she waits patiently for me to answer her.

"I'm a wine maker." I watch her eyes widen and her mouth opens and closes trying to get words out. I continue, "I'm in charge of the entire wine making process— sources, production, bottling, and selling. I own The Merlot Man in Manhattan."

I've always loved my work ever since I was a young boy. I had this fascination with what adults were drinking that I couldn't. My dad was the mayor of New York. Grand parties, galas, and public events around the city were a weekly thing for me. I had to sit in the corner and watch as he moved around the room, talking to every person. Pretending I wasn't there, I had to blend into the walls and be seen but not heard. Every person in any room I was in had a glass filled to the top with this strong-smelling liquid.

So, naturally, my curiosity peaked, and I remember the first time I tried some wine. The harsh, rich body trickled down my throat as the fruity after taste lingered on my tongue. I hated it. But each week, each event, I'd sip an assorted colour or smelling wine. By the time I had gotten to my teenage years, I'd tried most wines I could get my hands on. I would find myself researching unusual ways to make it and coming up with new flavours to make wine better.

Throwing her hands in the air, Brim beams at me. "That's *so* fucking cool!" She pops every word and I grin widely back at her. I huff a laugh and give my thanks. "What do you do, Fruit Loop?"

"Well, it's not as good as your job, but I'm a professional matchmaker." Now it's my turn to look at her wildly. She giggles and pulls at the bottom of her sweater. "My sisters and I started an online dating site where we set people up based on their preferences, interests, stars signs, aspirations in life." She waves her hand in front of her face. "Based on anything, really."

"Wow" I nod my head in surprise. Who'd have thought the Christmas tree hugger was a match maker?

She bites her lower lip and furrows her brows. "You seem speechless," she comments quietly.

I nod. "Yeah, I kind of am, I guess. I just figured you were a cookie maker or Santa's little helper." She barks out a laugh, bringing music to my ears.

"You said sisters; how many do you have?"

She nods, looking down at her sweater again. "I have five sisters. No brothers— it was a house full of girls at one point for dad."

Shit, mommy and daddy didn't own a tv by the sounds of it. "Five sisters? Jesus, that's a lot. I only have one younger brother, Jack. My parents were hoping for one of each. I'd have loved a little sister, I think."

Brim's about to reply to me when our narrator pipes up again. "So, the courtship display has finally begun. The male opens up, showing the female he does have a heart, after all. Maybe he can attract this strong female."

Brim slaps her hand over her face and her cheeks turn pink. I mouth it's okay silently to her and rub my thumb over the back of her hand like she did for me.

We chat a little while longer, sipping our wine handed to us by the air hostess, and I must admit, it has been a while since I've had a normal conversation with a woman. Well, anyone for that matter. I explain the process of tasting wine to her, and she tells me all about her sisters: Rory, Annie, Francesca, Abbey, and Lottie. I get the feeling though halfway through our chat Brim wasn't good with alcohol and might be tipsy off one glass.

"Let's play a game," she says, while flopping into the side of me. She looks up at my face and her eyes are glossy, while her pupils are dilated.

I smile down at her. "Shouldn't you try sleeping?" Pouting at me, she points a finger in my direction. "No, I wanna play a game." I laugh at her child-like response and answer her in quick defeat. "Okay, Fruit Loop, what's the game?"

"Puns! Christmas puns— the aim of the game is to fit in as many Christmas puns as possible for the rest of the flight. The one with the most at the end is the winner, simple."

"That's stupid, and no to Christmas," I answer, shuffling uncomfortably in my seat.

Arguing back, she angrily asks, "What's your deal with Christmas anyway? It's the most wonderful time of year."

"For some, yeah, it might be but for others it isn't, okay, Brimley?" My sharp tone was completely unwarranted, I know that, but I can't help it. The cheery disposition and naivety sets me on edge.

"Frosty the snowman's personal affairs are snow-body's business," the lady with the Dictaphone calls out. Brim starts uncontrollably laughing, setting me off too. Brim calls back, "Icy what you did there," gaining a few more laughs from other passengers seated nearby.

I stop laughing and turn my face serious. "It's snow joke, Fruit Loop." I wink at her for good measure.

"Ahhhhhh! He came, he thawed, he conquered," comes from behind me. I turn to see an old couple grinning at Brim and me, and I shake my head back and forth. You know the saying, *if you can't beat them, join them.*

"Yeah, well, I'm holding on for deer life here," I grumble back and glance at Brim. She's eyeing me curiously and nibbling the inside of her cheek. Without thinking, I lean across the seat and rub her jaw line, feeling tingles rush through my fingers. I quickly pull my hand away and remind myself I don't know her. I'm still unsure why I'm so comfortable around her.

Leaning back into my seat, I close my eyes, listening to the narrator, the old man behind me, and Brim as they drop some more puns, before darkness takes over and I drift off to sleep.

***

Read the rest here https://amzn.eu/d/0geRRnf

What's to Come.

First, let us talk LFTH series ...

Book 4 in the Letters From The Heart (LFTH) series, it is time for Max to have her say, don't you think? (Wink emoji) coming 2025.

Nate's story (Book 5 – LFTH series) as you know was due to come out October 2024 in a military anthology, but this was pushed back to 2025 –follow my Instagram to keep up to date on this release.

———

If you have been following my socials, you will have seen, I have a runaway bride meets ranch owner story called **Love on The Run** coming February 14, 2025.

I cannot wait for you to meet Hannah and Mason in this small town, unexpected love rom-com.

These two might have broken my heart and taken the lead as my favourite couple written to date.

More news to come on that soon.

———

And lastly, you have been asking and so, so patient for it ….(Insert drum roll)

Book 2 and 3 of the ***Into the Woods Trilogy*** will be out in 2025 as well. (WHOOP LOUDLY)

Alpha Asher and Elara have been hard freaking work to talk to (understatement of the year—trust me), but they are back and ready to finish their epic love story.

I have a few more books in the works, so follow my socials for more updates.

***

Acknowledgements

For – Dashing Through The Snow

My readers and supporters – *Without you, I would not be here. Thank you for your time, shares, comments, and likes and for your continued love.*

Colby, my editor – *Thank you for being the star you are, and supporting me the way you do! You are one of a kind, the attention the detail, love and care you put into each of my manuscripts, means so much to me. I cannot thank you enough nor will I ever stop raving about you to others.*

Tasha – *Honestly what would I do with out you! You are the go to girl every author needs! Thank you for taking the time to look over DTTS, your advise, and thoughts helped me shine up my script. I love you.*

Forever After PR – *Thank you for asking me to become a part of your amazing team. Without your love and dedication these last few months, I am 100% certain I would have crashed and burned out. Thank you so much for your time and patience. Here is to many more books. (Insert glass of wine emoji)*

Love Notes PR – *Thank you so much Ellie for all your hard work and love, but mostly thank you for having the patience of a saint while i asked you a million and one questions through random emails. Cannot wait to work with you again in the future.*

My Family —*Thank you for your never-ending love and support. Thank you. I love you all more than words can say.*

About the Author

Laura Rush is 31 years old, released her debut novel, Yours Truly, mid-2023.

She lives in North Yorkshire, UK with her husband, son, and dog.

Laura writes rom-com romances with smut.

When she is not writing, you'll find her sipping martinis, spending time with her family, reading a book, or going for long walks.

You can find me on:

Facebook @authorlaurarush

Instagram @authorlaurarush

TikTok @authorlaurarush

Printed in Great Britain
by Amazon